DEADLY
SOUTHERN
CHARM

DEADLY SOUTHERN CHARM

A LETHAL LADIES MYSTERY ANTHOLOGY

EDITED BY

MARY BURTON
AND MARY MILEY

WILDSIDE PRESS

Published by
Wildside Press, LLC.
wildsidepress.com

CONTENTS

INTRODUCTION, by Mary Burton and Mary Miley 7

THE GIRL IN THE AIRPORT, by Frances Aylor 9

MOURNING GLORY, by Mollie Cox Bryan 17

CAYCE'S TREASURES, by Lynn Cahoon 28

KEEPSAKES, by J.A. Chalkley 38

SOUTHERN SISTERS STICK TOGETHER, by Stacie Giles 49

THE POWER BEHIND THE THRONE, by Barb Goffman 58

STEWING, by Libby Hall 67

SHADOW MAN, by Brad Harper 76

COUNTRY SONG GONE WRONG, by Sherry Harris 82

KEEP YOUR FRIENDS CLOSE, by Maggie King 92

UNBRIDLED, by Kristin Kisska 101

DEADLY DEVONSHIRE, by Samantha McGraw 112

BURN, by K.L. Murphy 120

WHO KILLED BILLY JOE?, by Genilee Swope Parente 129

A JOB TO DIE FOR, by Deb Rolfe 138

JUST LIKE JIMINY CRICKET, by Ronald Sterling 149

NEVER MARRY A REDHEAD, by S.E. Warwick 154

ART ATTACK, by Heather Weidner 163

ABOUT THE AUTHORS 171

ABOUT THE EDITORS 173

INTRODUCTION

Ever since colonial days, the American South has captivated the imagination of the world with its vaunted reputation for charm. Early visitors praised the gracious manners of its people; travelers were enchanted by the warm hospitality they received; outsiders envied the romance of the moonlight-and-magnolias culture. Yet there has always been a dark side to this cheerful image of the South, a deadly underbelly of violence, tales half-told, and people who vanish into the night. This is the realm of *Deadly Southern Charm*.

Each story in this collection features a Southern woman, past or present, who illustrates that paradoxical mixture of femininity and fortitude known as the steel magnolia. Who could imagine a gently bred Southern lady capable of solving a murder or, for that matter, wielding the dagger herself? Bless her heart.

Our short stories are, of course, set in the South. They may take place on an old plantation, in a struggling small town, or in the distant reaches of a bayou. They may involve murder, haunts, mysteries, or just plain creepy encounters. Each story contains ingredients that give the South its unique flavor—its dialect and quirky speech patterns, for example, or its emphasis on family. And what Southern tale lacks an eccentric character? From many entries, the editors selected the most unusual, the most imaginative, and the very best for your enjoyment. We would also like to give a special thanks to our published guest authors, Mollie Cox Bryan, Lynn Cahoon, Barb Goffman and Sherry Harris for contributing stories to the collection.

Take one at bedtime. It will bring—if not *sweet* dreams, vivid ones.

Best,

Mary Burton and Mary Miley

THE GIRL IN THE AIRPORT

FRANCES AYLOR

If my flight hadn't been delayed, I would never have witnessed the murder.

The storm system had hit Atlanta around three o'clock that afternoon and was part of a wide mass of squalls that muscled in from the Atlantic and quickly smothered the entire East Coast. Powerful winds slammed against the airport terminal as churning black clouds dumped torrential rains onto the tarmac. The *on time* flight notices on the departure board flipped to *delayed*—first one, then three, then all the rest, succumbing one after another like helpless victims of a particularly contagious strain of flu.

Passengers groaned, grabbing their phones to alert friends and co-workers of the delay. Then, as people tend to do when under stress, they grabbed their belongings and headed for the nearest bar.

The last thing I needed was more alcohol. My head was still fuzzy from last night's fraternity party. I was still wearing my favorite sundress and the boots that stuck to the beer-slicked floor as I had danced for hours celebrating the end of my sophomore year of college and the survival of the world, which hadn't imploded months ago when we had flipped the calendar to Y2K.

But the smell of grilled meat and fried onions teased my stomach, reminding me that it had been a long time since breakfast, so I followed the crowd. The restaurant was packed, every table taken, the aisles blocked with roller bags and duffels. I threaded my way to the counter and ordered a Coke.

I felt a tap on my shoulder. "I'm Nora and my sister, Grace, and I have an extra chair at our table. Come join us."

Nora was a big-boned, lumbering, middle-aged gal. She had frizzy hair colored an unfortunate shade of orange thanks to a botched home-dye job.

She looked harmless enough, but as a woman traveling by myself, I was wary of strangers. I tightened my feet around the backpack.

"We are going to England too," she said as she nodded to the British Isles guidebook poking out of my backpack. "Grace and I are embarking on a two-week Jane Austen tour."

My head pounded and my stomach grumbled. It would be nice to sit down. "Great. I'm Robbie."

Nora held up well-worn copy of *Pride and Prejudice*. "Have you read this?"

"No."

"You should give Jane a try. She's such a shrewd judge of character. You coming?"

My beer-stained boots were starting rub against a blister I had worn last night. What harm could it do to sit with the sisters for a half hour? "Sure."

"My sister and I have read each of Jane's books three times," Nora said proudly. "Isn't that right, Grace?"

Grace was plump and petite, with dark bangs hanging low over her eyes. She looked nothing like her sister. She glanced up from a paperback sporting a bodice-ripper cover featuring a shirtless man with six-pack abs embracing a busty young woman whose chestnut curls cascaded over her shoulders.

"Yes we have," Grace said.

"Is that an Austen book?" I asked.

"Oh, no," Grace said, blushing. "This is a little something I picked up here at the airport. Change of pace."

"Pure trash," Nora said, shaking her head. "Little sisters. What are you gonna do?"

I decided right then I had made a mistake. I now risked spending the next couple of hours listening to these middle-aged women talk about Jane Austen. But a quick glance around convinced me there wasn't anywhere else to sit. When a man from behind me reached for my chair, I sat down.

As I settled, I realized there was another woman with them. She was a thin blonde trying to dress a lot younger than her age, wearing snug royal blue pants and a sleeveless white cotton sweater that showed off tan, muscular arms.

"This is Meredith, from Charleston," Nora said. "We met her earlier in the bookstore, and she was gracious enough to let us share her table. Meredith, this is Robbie."

"Lovely to meet you, Robbie," Meredith said.

Meredith reminded me of several of my mother's overachiever friends. She had that confident monied look of a woman who organized charity fundraisers, served as president of her garden club, played a mean game of tennis, and in her spare time, tutored underprivileged children at the local elementary school.

"Grace and I are going to fight our way to the counter to order some food," Nora said. "Can we bring you two something?"

"Nothing for me, thanks," Meredith said, gesturing toward her empty salad bowl. "I've already eaten."

I pulled a crumpled twenty from my pocket. "I'm starving. I'd love a barbecue and onion rings."

Nora raised a hand in protest. "We'll cover this, honey. You save your money for your trip."

"Thanks, but you don't need to do that."

"Our treat," Nora insisted. "We'll be right back."

I pushed my backpack under the table. "Thanks."

Picking up her wine, Meredith smiled. "Tell me, Robbie, where are you headed?" She very deliberately wrapped her tongue around each word of her Southern drawl, the way I'd done at parties when I knew I'd had too much to drink but was hoping no one else would notice.

"I'm meeting my cousin, Sarah, in England. We are backpacking through England, Wales and Ireland." Sarah, a history professor and genealogy buff, had offered to foot the bill if I would join her to help research our family tree. While weeks spent digging into dusty church records and rambling through ancient cemeteries wasn't exactly my top choice for a summer vacation, it seemed the only way I could afford a European trip, making it an irresistible offer.

"Sounds like fun," she said.

"Yep."

"You don't seem too excited. I remember my first summer in Europe. I couldn't wait to get on the plane."

"I *am* excited. It's just that…" I paused.

"Let me guess. There's a boyfriend involved. And he doesn't want you to go. Am I close?"

"Not exactly." If only Nate had demanded that I stay. But after spending almost every day with me for months, he had suddenly lost interest and transferred all his attention to my roommate, Fontaine. I pretended I was fine with the two of them hanging out night after night in a dark corner of the library. But inside I was in agony, losing sleep, skipping class, and barely squeaking through my econ finals. How could I think about the Laffer curve or the

Keynesian cross or maximizing expected utility when my heart was breaking? It was a relief to finally blurt out the truth. "My boyfriend, Nate, dumped me for my best friend. It seemed like a good time to leave town."

Meredith nodded sympathetically. "That's a tough one. What happened?"

I had spent a lot of sleepless pre-dawn hours trying to figure it out. It wasn't that she was prettier than me. We looked a lot alike, both of us were tall with long dark hair. Freshman year, people even thought we were sisters. We were both athletic—I had a killer serve in volleyball; she was a star on the lacrosse team. And we both liked to joke around. I would tell funny stories about what happened in class, and she would laugh so hard that she'd snort milk out of her nose.

The real reason had to be money. Fontaine's dad had a big job at a Fortune 500 company. Her family had vacation houses and trust funds. My dad died when I was fifteen, leaving behind a small insurance policy and a long list of debts. Nate was as poor as I was. Fontaine's wealth drew him like ants to a picnic. "She's rich. I'm not."

"Men can be so stupid," Meredith said. "Always chasing sex or money or both. Believe me, better to find out the truth about Nate now than after you've spent your whole life trying to please him. And then he dumps you anyway for some young floozy."

It sounded like she was talking from personal experience. "Your husband did that?" I asked.

"Yes. She's half his age. Younger than our children. And he's making a complete fool of himself over her." She shrugged. "Ours was a typical story. I worked to put him through pharmacy school, and then stayed home with the children while he built his empire. I used to think, 'Poor dear works so hard.' He was never at home, always traveling to visit his string of drug stores that he finally sold to one of those mega-chains for big bucks. And then I found out he had been doing more than working during his travels. He'd been having an affair with one of his pharmaceutical sales reps. Divorced me and now plans to marry her."

She was giving me a lot more details than I really wanted to hear, but I was stuck until Nora and Grace came back with our food. "I'm sorry."

"Don't be. I'm better off without him. And the good thing is, he doesn't have anywhere near the money she thinks he does." She leaned forward, glancing around to see if anyone else was listening. "It's amazing how many assets you can get your hands on when you have a clever lawyer and a determined forensic accountant," she whispered. "I got the Mercedes, the river place, his antique car collection, his race horses and half his stock portfolio. Plus our house and everything in it, including his own special stash of exotic pharmaceuticals." Her laugh was bitter. "She gets him. I got the better deal."

It made me feel a little better about losing Nate. As much as I loved him, I knew he was the restless type who would always struggle to be faithful. Maybe it was better to split up now than have my heart broken again and again.

"To lost loves," Meredith said, raising her glass.

I nodded as Nora and Grace came back to our table. "They're really backed up, but the waitress promised she'd bring our food over as soon as possible," Nora said.

"We can squeeze in one more, can't we?" Grace asked. "This is Shelby. We met her also in the bookstore earlier today. She's another Jane Austen fan."

Shelby's long blond curls reminded me of the woman on the cover of Grace's bodice ripper. She was maybe thirty-five, dressed in a shimmering peach tank top and white stretch pants.

"Shelby's heading to the Caribbean, Meredith," Grace said. "To visit her fiancé."

Shelby settled into a chair, setting her glass of red wine on the table. "I was supposed to go down there yesterday, but I had this project I had to finish for work first. And now with this stupid weather, my flight's delayed. Just my luck."

"But once you get there, it will be wonderful," Grace said, her eyes bright as she glanced at the rest of us. "Shelby's story is so romantic. She fell in love with an older man who is funny and kind and best of all, rich. It's like what Jane Austen said. You remember, Nora, that first line from *Pride and Prejudice*?"

"Of course," Nora said. "'It is a truth universally acknowledged, that a single man in possession of a good fortune, must be in want of a wife.'" She smiled. "Shelby, tell us all about him."

"There's not a lot to tell. As Grace said, he's quite a bit older than I, which made me shy away from him for a long time. But he was so persistent. Sent me flowers. Took me out to dinner. We spent a long weekend in the Bahamas. And now we're meeting in St. Lucia."

"He's a widower?" Nora asked.

"No. He's recently divorced from a real tyrant of a wife. I've never met her, of course, but from what Carl says, she's quite a cold fish. After all, men don't wander when their wives keep them satisfied, right?"

Meredith coughed, her face turning bright red.

"Are you okay?" I asked, patting her on the back.

She nodded as she cleared her throat. "Yes. My wine went down the wrong way."

The waitress finally brought our food and drinks. "I already know I'll need another Coke," I said. "Parched."

"And I'll have another ginger beer," Nora said.

"Refills all around?" the waitress asked.

"Yes. A coffee for me," Grace said. "And Shelby, what are you having? A cabernet?"

"No. Merlot."

Nora and Grace entertained us with stories of Jane Austen characters while we ate. After a while the waitress returned, carefully balancing a large tray. She had just set my second soda in front of me when someone at the table behind her stood up, his chair smacking hard against her hips. The tray tipped, splashing coffee, red wine and ginger beer all over Grace, Shelby, and Nora.

"You idiot," Shelby snapped. She mopped at her peach top with a handful of napkins. "You'll lose your job over this. I want to see the manager, right now."

"Shelby, honey, surely you don't mean that?" Meredith said. "It was an accident. You ladies go freshen up, and I'll order a fresh round of drinks, on me."

The waitress gave Meredith a grateful smile as she wiped up the spreading liquid. She came back quickly with a new round of drinks. "No charge for these, ma'am," she said. "I'm so sorry. But it's really tight in here, what with everyone squeezed in. And grumpy because they've missed their connections."

"You don't need to explain, my dear," Meredith said. "It was obviously an accident. And those ladies have plenty of other outfits they can change into."

"You have such a calming influence on everyone," I said as the waitress walked away. "I'm not sure I would have handled that nearly as well."

"Things happen," she said simply.

I kept working on my onion rings as we waited for the others to come back. Finally Meredith said, "Robbie, dear, can you let them know our drinks are here? I can't imagine what's taking so long. Grace's coffee is getting cold."

"Of course." I headed down the hall to the ladies' room. About six women were outside the door, waiting to get in. They glared at me as I made my way around them. "Looking for my friends," I said apologetically. "Nora? Grace?" I called out. "You guys in here?"

Nora and Grace, now changed into new outfits, were standing in front of the sink drying their hands. "Meredith was getting worried about you." I looked around. "Where's Shelby?"

"Here I am," Shelby said, pushing open the door of the end stall. She tugged at her blouse as she approached the mirror. "I'm not happy about this. My top is ruined. That wine stain is never coming out." She was still grumbling as we returned to the table. "I can't believe that waitress was so stupid. I still think she should get fired."

Nora and Grace looked uncomfortable as they settled in beside her. "It could have happened to anyone," Nora said. "It *is* really crowded in here. I mean, I know it's terribly annoying, but I don't think it was her fault."

"We should at least get compensated for our ruined clothes," Shelby insisted. She quickly knocked back her Merlot.

"Why don't we focus on our vacations?" Grace said. "Think of the good times we're all going to have."

Nora picked up her ginger beer. "I'm really excited about our trip. We'll be staying at this quaint little hotel in Salisbury. The Red Lion. It dates back to the thirteenth century."

"And we'll visit the church where Jane Austen's father preached," Grace said. "And Montacute House, where *Sense and Sensibility* was filmed. And the gardens of Stourhead, used in the movie *Pride and Prejudice*."

"That's right," Nora said, nodding. "And then we'll finish up at Winchester Cathedral, where Jane is buried."

Shelby suddenly clutched her stomach. "I feel sick." She jumped up and headed for the restroom.

"What's that all about?" Grace asked, watching her sprint down the hall.

"Probably gulped her wine too fast," Meredith said. "That can really mess with your tummy."

The rest of us finished our meals while Nora and Grace shared more details of their trip. When Meredith signaled to the waitress for the bill, Grace said, "Shelby's been gone a long time. Maybe we should go check on her?"

Nora stood up. "Good idea. Let's make sure she's all right."

As they walked away, the blare of the intercom cut through the chatter of the diners. "Ladies and gentlemen, good news. The storm has tapered off, and we will resume our regular flights shortly. Please proceed to your assigned gates."

"About time," I said.

Meredith began to gather her belongings. "Thanks for letting me vent, Robbie. I get incredibly frustrated every time I think of my ex-husband. Can I show you his picture?"

"Sure." She handed me a dog-eared photo of a handsome older man and a much younger woman, their faces close together, her lips drawn in a sexy pout. "Meredith, this woman looks a lot like Shelby."

"She does, doesn't she?" She grinned. "My private investigator took that for me."

"Your private investigator?" I hesitated. "You knew she'd be on this flight?"

"No. But I knew Shelby was meeting Carl in St. Lucia. I had hoped to get there first with a little surprise for him. Some of those exotic pharmaceuticals that he was gracious enough to leave behind." Meredith picked up Shelby's empty glass and shoved it in her purse.

Just then we heard loud screaming from the direction of the restrooms. "Call 9-1-1," someone shouted.

"Meredith, what have you done?" I asked.

The older woman grinned. "It was nice to meet you, Robbie. I hope you have a lovely time in England. And forget about Nate. He sounds like nothing but trouble."

"Meredith, you can't get away with this. The police will catch up with you, even in St. Lucia."

Meredith stood up. "There's been a change of plans. I don't need to go to St. Lucia now." She pushed her roller bag into the aisle. "I think I'll head to Montenegro."

"Why Montenegro?"

She smiled. "It's a wonderful country. Delightful people. Beautiful beaches. And best of all... no extradition treaty with the U.S."

The screams had gotten louder. Security personnel rushed past me. I tried to flag them down, to point them toward Meredith, but they were too focused on responding to the tragedy to notice me.

Pinned in by the other diners, I soon lost sight of her as she disappeared into the crowd.

MOURNING GLORY

MOLLIE COX BRYAN
Guest Author

Nobody does funerals like Southerners. But in Victoria Town, Virginia, mourning was an art form. Steeped in its celebrated Victorian roots, the town's residents hung crape, wore black ribbons, and even donned Victorian mourning clothing when appropriate. Mourning Arts offered everything the modern Virginian in this quaint, historic village needed when a loved one passed.

Viv Barton stood in front of Mourning Arts, wondering why the black-fringed shades were still drawn and the closed sign dangled in the window. Hadn't Stu said 8:30? The door popped open and Stu, the manager, smiled. "Come on in!"

She entered the store, following the lanky, slightly hunched, Stu, as her first-day-of-work fears turned to edginess. She sucked in air. How hard could this be?

"You're a gamer, so you're familiar with computers. Think of the register as a computer, and you'll have no problem," Stu said. He led her through a lesson, then pulled out his pocket watch and checked the time. Viv couldn't decide if he was authentic or affected. His thin dark eyebrows rose. "We'll open in twenty minutes. Let's spruce things up."

The shop was one of the few Viv frequented in Victoria Town, so she was acquainted with it. Most of the other shops brimmed with rose and pink, lace, feathers, ornate woodwork. Not her taste. Stu handed her a bottle of glass cleaner and paper towels. "You can start by cleaning the cases."

He couldn't have given her a better job. Mourning jewelry was her passion. Today, she'd worn her favorite lover's eye mourning pendant with its tiny red garnets on a black velvet choker, a piece she'd inherited from her grandmother. As she wiped the glass, she admired the exquisite pieces on display. Mourning jewelry was more than hair and fingernails fashioned into pendants, bracelets, and rings. She approached the glass case with the famous Queen Victoria mourning set, on loan from a London museum to Mourning Arts. As Stu had intended, the special display lured people to Victoria Town and to his store. He'd been on the radio and television so often promoting it that Viv's Aunt Libby would roll her eyes at every occasion. She thought his self-promotion gauche.

"Are you done over there?" Stu asked, as he straightened crape garments along the wall.

Viv gave the counter one more swipe. "Yes."

He walked up to her and inspected her outfit. "I like that Victorian jacket with the black-and-white-striped corset. The blouse underneath, not so much. Next time, leave it at home."

Viv grimaced. She'd never wear the corset without a blouse during the day—at her job. What was wrong with him?

At 10 o'clock, Stu whispered that it was teatime. "Can I bring you a cup and some chocolate scones?"

"I don't drink hot tea," Viv said. She liked her tea sweet with plenty of ice. "But I'll take a scone." If she couldn't have her tea iced, she'd make do with water in her black, custom-made bottle with a skull and crossbones on it.

Stu carried in a tray and sat it on a tiny table behind the counter. Teatime was a ritual for him. He kept his sugar (or was it saccharin?) in a small, jewel-encrusted vial that he tapped with one bony finger until the clumps fell into his cup. He stirred in cream, brought his cup to his mouth, and sipped with obvious rapture. Viv turned away. Watching the pointy-chinned Stu slurp his tea gave her the creeps.

Stu's smile vanished as a man sporting a beard and a cane walked into the shop. He stood and started to scurry into the back room.

"I see you, my man," the stranger said, his voice booming. "You ripped me off. We need to talk."

"Ripped you off?" Stu turned to face him. His cheek twitched. "I paid you for your services." Flustered, his eyes moved between Viv and some browsers in the shop. "Shall we go in my office?"

"I don't think so, Stu," the man said. "I want a piece of the action, and I want it by midnight tonight." The intruder turned and lumbered out of the store.

"Who was that?" Viv asked, her heart thudding.

Stu shrugged. "Just some guy I know. Turns out he's crazy, but he makes the most beautiful jewelry." Viv turned away in embarrassment, wiping non-existent dust off the counter.

The rest of the morning passed without incident, with Stu popping in and out between the back of the shop and the front.

"I'm going out for a veggie burger," he said at noon. "Can I bring you one?" Stu said, his eyes shining.

There was no place in Victoria Town proper that carried veggie burgers—not that Viv knew about anyway. "Sure. Who has veggie burgers?"

He leaned in closer to her. "Who indeed?" he mocked with a mysterious tone of voice. He walked out the door with a slight sway. She couldn't understand what her pharmacist friend Abby saw in the man. He resembled a pale ostrich. But Abby was nuts about him. In fact, she was thrilled that Viv had gotten a job working with him—so she could watch over what Abby called his "flirtatious" nature.

A few women trickled into the shop and bought some pieces of the cheaper mourning jewelry. A man picked up a jacket he'd ordered earlier. But most people came by to view the prized Queen Victoria collection.

Then wouldn't you know it, her Aunt Libby came in. "Just peeking in to see how you're doing on your first day."

"You don't need to check up on me," Viv said. "I'm doing fine. Stu is so impressed, he left me in charge and went out for lunch."

Aunt Libby's eyebrows shot up. "Lunch? It's half past three."

Had time gone that quickly? "He must have gotten hung up." *Or maybe he drove to Richmond for those veggie burgers.*

But come 5 o'clock, Viv understood no veggie burger would be coming, and she closed the shop. Shaky and nervous, she told herself it was because she'd had no lunch.

Viv made her way down the cobblestone street past Feathers & Ruffles, past Fans and Parasols, past Elizabeth's Custom Corsets, and out of the cobbled town square to the paved street. She turned left and walked along the edge of the old cemetery bordered by an ornate black iron fence. Her Aunt Libby's pink bed & breakfast stood on the other side of the graveyard in a row of other, smaller Victorian houses with gingerbread woodwork, painted in historically accurate colors. Viv walked in the door of the B & B and smelled her aunt's spaghetti. Thank God. She was starving.

Later that night, before she drifted off to sleep, she wondered what had happened to Stu. Why did he leave her at Mourning Arts alone on her first day? A loud knocking interrupted her sleep. Was it morning already? She blinked the clock into view: 3:37. What was going on?

Viv untangled herself from the blankets. Aunt Libby was at her door, eyes ablaze.

"There's police officers downstairs. What have you gotten yourself into? Do I need to call a lawyer?"

"Calm down, Aunt Libby. I've done nothing wrong. Let me get my robe."

Aunt Libby followed her into the room. "I'm glad we've only one guest tonight. I hope he sleeps through this."

Viv slipped on her robe and made her way downstairs where two officers waited.

"Vivian Barton?" one officer asked as she came down the stairs.

"Yes, can I help you?"

"I'm Officer Willoughby and this is my partner Officer Thorncraft. We're sorry to disturb you at this time of night. But it couldn't be helped."

Aunt Libby and Viv sat down on the floral loveseat in the parlor; the officers sat on the blue velvet couch.

"Do you work at Mourning Arts?"

"She started yesterday," Libby said.

Viv elbowed her gently. She could answer her own questions.

"Yes," Viv said. Her brain hadn't quite kicked into gear.

"Do you know this man?" Officer Willoughby handed her a photo.

"Stu Johnson," Viv said. "The owner of the shop and my boss."

"We regret to inform you he's dead."

Aunt Libby gasped and placed her hands over her mouth. Viv's heart thudded against her chest. "What happened?" she asked, tears of shock pricking at her eyes. She reached for a tissue, embarrassed by her tears.

"We're not sure. We're hoping you can tell us about yesterday at the shop. You were working, correct?"

Viv nodded and blew her nose, composing herself. "He left to get us some veggie burgers for lunch and never came back. I wondered what happened to him."

"When you closed the shop, was anything out of place or missing?" Officer Willoughby asked.

"No, nothing."

"Sometime between 5 and midnight, when we found Mr. Johnson, Queen Victoria's jewelry disappeared from the shop."

"What?"

"If what you're saying is correct, the place was robbed after you left. Either that or you took the set," Officer Willoughby said.

Viv's heart raced.

"My niece is not a thief," Libby said, before she could respond herself. "And she's very bright. Would she steal a priceless item like that on her first day of work? Really!"

"I'm sorry to offend. You understand it's procedure. Just doing my job, Ms. Barton," Willoughby said.

"The jewels are gone?" Viv said. "We've got to find them. They belong to a museum in London. Stu jumped through hoops to bring them here. How did he die?"

"We're not sure. His body is with the medical examiner. It appears there was a struggle. Did you witness any arguments at the shop?" Willoughby asked.

"Yes, in fact there was one minor incident." Viv relayed what had happened with the jewelry maker.

"Did you catch this man's name?"

"No, I'm sorry. But it should all be on the security tape."

The officers gave one another meaningful glances. "Tell us everything that happened from the minute you walked into the shop yesterday."

After the police left, Viv climbed back in bed. Twenty-four hours ago, she couldn't sleep because she was so excited about her new job. Now, she was having a hard time sleeping because her boss was dead. And she was jobless.

Her cell phone woke her early.

"It's Abby. Have you heard?" She was sobbing. "Stu is dead!"

Viv struggled to find the right words. "The police told me in the middle of the night. It's awful. I'm so sorry, Abby."

"Can you come over?"

"I'll be there as soon as I can."

Abby's blue eyes were tiny slits in red puffiness. "We need to figure out what happened to him!" she cried when she saw Viv.

"The police are working on that. They're doing some tests to see what killed him."

Her wailing stopped for a moment and her chest heaved with a shuddering gasp. "He was kind of an oddball, but he was a good guy. I can't think of any reason someone would hurt him—unless it was a woman he'd rejected!"

"That's crazy talk. He may have walked in on a thief stealing the jewels."

Abby paced back and forth in her small studio apartment. "That would only make sense if he was shot or stabbed, right? The police said that he wasn't."

"Did he keel over and die? Maybe he had a heart attack. Please sit down, Abby. You're making me a nervous wreck."

"I've been telling him for months he needed a better security system… Proper cameras…" she said sitting on the edge of the couch, rubbing her hands on her jeans.

"Wait. He had cameras. I saw them."

"They're always broken," she said, her voice trailing off.

"I can't imagine a British museum would lend those jewels to a place that didn't have top-quality security. Maybe he'd gotten those cameras fixed."

"Victoria Town is one of the safest towns in the state. Perhaps in the country. The town hasn't had a major crime in years. Plus he played up the town name angle and the historical links. Good PR for both of them."

Viv didn't buy that. No one lent Queen Victoria's jewelry to an establishment with shoddy security. "Maybe he wasn't killed. Maybe he discovered the jewels were gone and had a heart attack. I know he was relatively young, but young people do have heart attacks."

An odd expression passed over Abby's face. "He was complaining of low energy." Her tone hinted at more to the story. So Viv sat in the quiet, knowing that Abby, who liked to fill quiet spaces with babble, would say more. "Oh my God!" Abby's hands went to her face. "We gave him a little concoction from the pharmacy! It wasn't anything too strong, but could that be it? Did I help kill my boyfriend?" Her hands trembled.

Viv ushered her to the couch. "Now, Abby, calm down. Just lie here a moment." She concentrated on keeping her voice as comforting as could be. But what exactly had she given him? Surely Abby was being paranoid.

Viv's cell phone buzzed—Aunt Libby. She picked up. "The police want to speak with you again. You're the last person who saw Stu alive."

Viv's brain kicked into gear. "Do they think I killed him?"

Abby sat up, mouth agape, eyes wide.

"I don't know, dear."

The police considered her a suspect? It was so ridiculous that it would be laughable if the matter were not so serious. Her heart thudded against her rib cage.

"Come home. They're here waiting on you," Aunt Libby said.

"But I'm with Abby and she's upset."

"Bring her along, then."

"You didn't kill him," Abby said as they walked along the edge of the cemetery fence. "So you have nothing to worry about."

"You didn't kill him either."

"I hope not."

Aunt Libby greeted them with a pot of hot cocoa and cookies. They went into the parlor where the police officers waited.

"We have a few more questions for you, Ms. Barton."

"Okay," Viv said, blowing on her cocoa to steady her nerves.

"Did you see anything odd yesterday in the shop?"

"You asked me that before, and I told you no. The day progressed in what I thought was a normal way. I was trained on the register, cleaned display cases, and waited on a few customers. Oh! Then Stu brought tea and chocolate scones from the back."

"You didn't mention that earlier."

"It was in the middle of the night. I was half asleep. I'm sorry."

Willoughby cleared his throat. "Did you drink the tea and eat the scone?"

"I never touch hot tea. Hate the stuff. But I ate the scone." Viv wondered where this was going.

"How did he take his tea?"

"With cream and sugar. He kept the sugar in a beautiful little vial."

The officers stood abruptly.

"Thank you. We'll be in touch. Please don't leave the area."

"This is where I live," Viv said. "Why would I leave?"

They left without answering. The three women sat silently for a while in the lavender room, the scent of hot cocoa mingling with potpourri and sunlight streaming through the lace curtain creating patterns on the wood floor.

"They must want to question you again," Aunt Libby said. "I hope this all works out soon. I'm expecting a full house this week. What will the guests think?"

That night, as Viv tossed and turned beneath her blankets, a pang of guilt tore through her. She was here to help Aunt Libby, not make things worse. She was the wayward-gamer-techie daughter and niece, who dressed in what they all considered weird clothing and sported several tattoos. But she loved her aunt and would do anything for her. She hoped it would be business as normal soon. That night, she dreamed of Stu, pale, falling, and reaching out to her.

Viv awoke with a shudder and stared up at her pink satin canopy. She'd never liked it. But this was the only available room. The canopy always reminded her of a coffin—tonight more than ever.

Viv glanced at the clock—5:30—pulled the chain on the lamp, and picked up her book. She needed to clear her mind. She knew she had nothing to do with Stu's death, and she would not let the police rattle her. No, they should investigate what happened—not bother her and Abby. Poor girl loved him so much it bordered on delusion. She tried to read, but questions kept pulling her thoughts away from the book. Where had Stu's body been found? Exactly how did he die? And what had happened to Queen Victoria's mourning jewels? How did Stu get them into the country without having proper security?

After breakfast, she dialed Abby. "Can you meet me at the shop?"

"Are you crazy? No. Let's stay away from there until the police figure this all out."

"Okay. You're either with me or not. I'm going in. I left my water bottle there, so if anybody catches me, I'll use it as an excuse."

Abby sighed. "What do you hope to accomplish?"

"I'm not sure. But I'd like to start by studying Stu's files about Queen Victoria's jewels."

"Okay," Abby said, her voice almost a whisper. "I'll meet you there."

They entered through the front door as if they had every right to be there. Which we do, thought Viv. In Stu's office they found papers and files on his desk, along with the tea set he'd used the day before. Viv opened the file cabinet, checking under "V" for Victoria. Nothing. Then she checked under "Q" for queen. Nothing.

"How would he file the jewels?"

"Maybe under J?"

"Brilliant!" Viv said, as she opened another drawer and found a pink folder with the word. "Jewelry" on it.

Documents detailing the history of several of the jewelry pieces in the shop were jammed into a manila folder. Viv sifted through it, searching for something on the jewels from Great Britain as Abby rummaged around on his desk.

"Shoot. I see nothing here about the jewels."

"Maybe he has the paperwork at his apartment," Abby said.

"Do you have a key?"

"No, sorry. We never went to his house. Stu always said he liked my place better."

So much for Viv's brief foray into sleuthing. Abby burst into another fit of sobs and Viv made her sit down. As she searched for a tissue, something caught her eye in the trash. Something black and shiny. "Oh my God, Abby, it's the jewels! They are right here. In the trash!"

"Wait!" Abby said. "Touch nothing!"

Viv's heart nearly stopped. Abby was right. "We should call the police."

"What are we going to tell them? I mean, we shouldn't even be here."

"Abby, these jewels are priceless. I don't think the police will care about us sneaking in here." Viv held up her water bottle. "We'll tell them I came for this."

Abby scooted around in her seat. "It's not a good idea. Let them find the jewels on their own."

What was wrong with her? She wasn't thinking straight. Viv dug her cell phone out of her purse. "We're calling the police right now."

"Looks like the robbery was interrupted, and they panicked," said Officer Willoughby a few minutes later. "We must get a forensics team in here. We'll need to fingerprint you both because you've been in here. You came for a water bottle?" He rolled his eyes.

Viv held it up. "It's special."

"Yeah. I can see that." He placed his hands on his hips.

"Please be careful with the jewelry," Viv said. "It's Queen Victoria's mourning set. Or one of them anyway."

Willoughby shrugged. "I thought mourning jewelry was about hair."

"Yes, some of it. But Queen Victoria also wore jet pieces during her many years of mourning Prince Albert," Viv said.

"I can't believe this is happening!" Abby sobbed. "Please find who killed my Stu!"

Willoughby shifted his weight. "We're doing our best, ma'am. We've gotten leads on two outsiders milling about that night."

"Tourists?" Viv asked.

"That's what we're trying to determine," he said. "But they may be our robbers. Or murderers."

A dapper gentleman walked into Stu's office. "Ladies, this is John Ainsworth. He's a jewelry and antiquities expert from the University of Virginia. We thought it was a good idea for him to examine the jewels and make certain we're storing them correctly."

"Cool," Viv said. Hard to place an age on him. His thick hair was gray and distinguished, but his face appeared younger.

The man held up the jet necklace to the light. "Fake," he said bluntly.

"What? How can that be?" Abby squealed.

Viv's mind swirled in confusion.

"I was suspicious when we found them in the trash," Willoughby said.

Ainsworth's eyebrows hitched. "I'd say you have one angry thief."

Abbey sobbed again. "Poor Stu, killed over fake jewelry!"

The room silenced. "That's one possibility," Ainsworth said. "But jewel thieves, as a rule, are not murderers. I gather this was more of a smash and grab, not a professional job."

"If that were the case, how would they know it was a fake? This is a well-made replica. It makes no sense," Willoughby said.

"Where are the papers?" Ainsworth said. "If these jewels came from a museum in London, they would have papers with them, detailing the loan."

"We've not found anything like that."

"Keep looking," he said, glancing at Abby and Viv. "May I speak with you in private, officer?"

Willoughby nodded. "It's time for you two to leave."

"Oh," Viv said, standing. "Sorry. Yes. I hope this all works out."

"I can't believe Stu was ripped off," Abby said, sniffing, as they walked out of the shop. "He was brilliant."

No he wasn't, Viv mused. Love is blind, but was it deaf and dumb too?

"Abby, you need to get a hold of yourself. I know it's hard losing someone. It's hard to imagine, but things will get better with time. I promise you."

"I loved him so much... and he loved me. Only me."

The next morning, commotion erupted from downstairs at the B&B. Viv could hear Aunt Libby say, "Do you have to come here? Can't you take her to the station and question her? I have a business to run."

Duly scolded, Willoughby cleared his throat. "I'm sorry. I'll just take a few minutes."

"Officer Willoughby," Viv said as she walked into the room, tying her robe. "What can I help you with?"

He held out a vial. "Is this the vial you saw Stu Johnson use when he added something to his tea?"

"Yes."

"It wasn't sugar. We've gotten the tox reports back. It was a common pick-me-up from the pharmacy, except there was a little something added to it. A poison derived from morning glory."

Viv's breath caught in her throat. How could that be? Abby mentioned making him something. She was a pro. She didn't make mistakes like that. "I don't understand. He was poisoned? By a jewel thief?"

"The jewels were fake from the start. He hired a man to forge them."

"What?" Viv's mind reeled, trying to make sense of all of this. Poison? Forgery?

"It was a publicity stunt!" Aunt Libby said. "I'm not surprised."

"So there was no thief?" Viv asked.

He shook his head.

"What will happen to the shop?" When it came out of her mouth, she realized how stupid it sounded. This probably wasn't the right question to ask. She struggled to find words. "I mean…"

"Don't worry. His wife will take care of the shop. It all belongs to her now."

CAYCE'S TREASURES

LYNN CAHOON
Guest Author

Strolling down the empty sidewalk, Cayce Andrews felt the heat with every step. Seattle was wet, but in New Orleans, the humidity was also hot and sticky, even in the early morning. Cups and trash littered the street, left over from a nightly French Quarter party.

As she crossed Royal Street in front of an old brick building, she saw a sidewalk sleeper eyeing her warily. She pulled a ten out of her tote. How the guy actually slept with all that going on, she didn't know. She'd bought earplugs for her move into her new apartment.

"I'm not doing nothing," the man mumbled as she moved toward the doorway. "You are here way too early. Customers don't show up until after ten."

"Who's been here?" She held out the bill, hoping the gaunt man would use it for a meal.

His dirt caked hand grabbed the money. Ignoring her question, he focused on something over her shoulder. Following his gaze, Cayce saw a police cruiser easing down the one-way street. She turned back to see the man had stuffed his few belongings onto a small rollaway cart and was already shuffling in the opposite direction.

"So much for chatting." Cayce focused on the building in front of her: 700 Royal, her building.

The joy and challenges of running a business in the historic New Orleans neighborhood had become her concern yesterday at two o'clock when she'd handed Matthew Goldstein a check. Owning an antique shop in the heart of NOLA had been her childhood dream.

A black Range Rover stopped in front of the building, and her brother stepped out. Nicolae Ardronic paused, his dark eyes taking in the building's rundown façade. He reached down and picked up an empty go-cup. "This is what you got for your inheritance from Grandmother Andrews? Having buyer's remorse yet?"

"Not on your life, Nic. I'm looking forward to starting this new chapter." Cayce couldn't help but grin at her brother. She dug the key out of her tote. "Want to see the inside?"

"Why not? My first appointment isn't until noon." Nic threw the cup into an overflowing trashcan. "I don't want you staying late here. You call me if you leave after dark."

"Funny, I found my way home for ten years in Seattle all by myself. Besides, by next week, I'll be living above the shop." Cayce fit the key into the lock and turned. She pushed but the door didn't move. She'd heard the lock click. "That's weird."

Nic held his hand out. "Let me try. These old buildings can be stubborn."

"I can do it myself." Cayce kept the sigh internal. Her big brother was always trying to take care of her. She turned the key again. He held up one hand as she pushed the door open an inch.

"Hold on. You don't think it was left open, do you?" He tried to peer into the shop without moving forward. "Who else has keys to this old firetrap?"

"That I don't know. But I'll find out." She pushed past him into the main showroom. The lights were on? The smell of dust and age surrounded her. "Hello? Is someone here?"

An older woman stepped out of a side room. "Good morning. You're my first customers of the day. What can I help you find?"

"Who are you?" Cayce asked.

The woman blinked in confusion. "I'm Sarah Stiner. And who am I helping today?"

"I'm Cayce Andrews. I purchased this building and the antiques business yesterday from Mr. Goldstein." Cayce believed in ripping off the Band-Aid. Apparently Goldstein hadn't taken care of the details like he'd promised.

The woman's eyes widened. "Matthew sold the store?"

"Yes." Cayce heard a noise from the back. "Who else is here?"

Sarah Stiner shook her head. "No one. I open the store Mondays through Fridays exactly at eight. I don't work weekends. I just saw him yesterday. Why wouldn't he have told me?"

Cayce was wondering the same thing. "I heard a noise in the back. Are you sure there's no one else here?"

"That's probably Harry." Sarah sank into a chair and closed her eyes. "I've worked here for over ten years. What am I going to do now?"

Cayce threw an exasperated glance at Nic. He stood across the room, focused intently on an antique lamp that would keep him out of the conversation.

"Who's Harry?" Cayce put a hand on the woman's shoulder, trying to calm her down. "Can I get you a glass of water?"

Sarah pulled a tissue from her pocket and wiped her face. "That would be nice. The break room's at the back, past the offices. Harry, well, he's the building's ghost."

Of course, there was a ghost rumor. The brick building dated back to the eighteenth century. Every property had at least one ghost story that the tourist trade used for the nightly ghost tours. "I'll go get the water."

"Cayce, be careful. She's not wrong." Nic called from across the shop. Apparently he had been listening. Cayce tried not to roll her eyes in front of her brother. He had inherited the clairvoyant gene that ran in the family. Sometimes she thought she had received a little of the gift, too.

She found her way to the door marked Employees Only. Apparently, Matthew Goldstein had been a little too excited about his big payoff to deal with his employees yesterday. Cayce would get hold of him today and have him speak with the rest of the staff. She'd rather hire her own crew than inherit staff loyal to the aging dealer.

For the first time, she wondered if coming home to New Orleans had really been the best idea. There were plenty of other cities where she could have bought an antiques business, probably for less. Instead, she'd been drawn home with all the consequences.

She passed two empty offices and paused at the one before the break room. The gold plate on the door read Matthew Goldstein. Maybe he's fallen asleep at his desk, she thought.

Pushing the door open, Cayce froze. A body lay before her, sprawled on a Persian rug stained crimson with blood. Matthew Goldstein wasn't going to be telling his employees anything about the shop's sale.

* * * *

"Are you positive the sale was completed?" Detective Boone Charles asked Cayce for the third time. He looked like a kid all dressed up for Halloween in his dad's suit. His blue eyes twinkled in a face that seemed younger than his age. She'd been sitting in the employee break room for the last hour, drinking coffee and going over the events that had led her to purchase the store. Her hand was steadier now, but every time she closed her eyes, she saw the body sprawled on the Persian rug.

"I handed him a check. We signed the documents. The title company was filing all the paperwork. The transfer was complete." Cayce glanced over to where Nic sat, working on his phone. He'd cancelled his appointments for the day to stay with her. Sarah Stiner had been questioned and let go thirty minutes ago.

"Then we'll be in touch," said the detective. The coroner had taken the body to the morgue and the crime scene guys had finished their work. Detective Charles closed his notebook and handed her a card. "I've written down the items we took out of Mr. Goldstein's office. This is your receipt, although I don't think you're going to want that rug back."

"So you're done here? We can clean up and open?" Cayce took the card and dropped it into her tote. "I've got to get the apartment upstairs ready for my stuff. The moving guys are coming next week."

"Please don't tell me you want to do that today." Nic didn't look up from his phone.

"Give it a day before you reopen, just in case we need to come back," said Detective Charles. He held his hand out to Cayce. "Sorry that your first day home turned into such a disaster." He smiled at her confused look. "You probably don't remember me, but we graduated high school together."

"Boone Charles? Math geek, right? Sure, I remember now. And it's not my first day back—I've been here for a few weeks, staying at the Monteleone." Cayce did remember him—a shy kid who blended into the crowd. He was cute but really not her type, then or now. She was addicted to bad boys, a habit she was determined to break. "Anyway, thanks for coming, Detective Charles."

"Call me Boone. My mother is only one who calls me Detective." Boone headed out the door. "It's a shame you've had this trouble."

Nic waited for the detective to leave before he spoke. "Any way I can talk you into coming back to the compound with me? Annamae would love to have you come for dinner."

"I don't think so. I just want to order room service and dig into this inventory. This is not how I'd planned to spend my first day. You can drop me off at the hotel though." She followed him out to the hallway, pausing at the door to Goldstein's office. "Help me look for the accounting records before we go."

Thirty minutes later, they'd gone through the office without finding much of anything. Nic closed the door behind them. "Maybe the police took his electronics."

Cayce nodded and headed to the door. "I guess so. I'll look more closely tomorrow." As she passed by the second office, her instincts told her to reach for the knob. Reason number four hundred and five that she shouldn't have come home: her own psychic powers were resurfacing. "Wait a sec. I might as well check this room out."

A white envelope sat on a laptop on a Queen Anne desk in the middle of the room. She read the letter inside. "It's from Mr. Goldstein. He says he loaded all the records on this laptop for me, and he'll be out of the larger office by the end of the week."

"He was off on his estimation by a few days." Nic picked up the laptop for her. "Let's get out of here."

Cayce followed him out to the doorway where she locked and double-checked the doors. Tomorrow she'd have the locks changed. There was too much riding on this venture for her to fail.

* * * *

After Nic dropped her off at the hotel, Cayce ordered room service and grabbed a new notebook from her stash. Some people used their phones for reminders. She liked paper lists.

As Matthew had promised, the laptop contained records of current employees, purchases, and sales for the last twenty years. Reviewing the statements, she quickly determined that he'd been losing money for years. The sample records he'd provided prior to the sale hadn't told the full story. Now she needed to build her business plan using the facts. Cayce started making lists.

Room service arrived right as she was getting ready to unwrap the candy bar on her desk. The smell of the holy trinity—onion, green pepper, and celery in the shrimp jambalaya—made her stomach growl. She poured herself a cup of half cocoa and half coffee and went back to her desk.

An hour later, the food was gone, the pots were empty, and Cayce had pages of questions with no answers. Like, why had Sarah been paid three times more in base salary than any other sales clerk, especially since her actual commissions were few and far between? And who was this Arnold Barnett who had an even larger salary? No wonder Matthew hadn't been making money. He was drowning in employee costs. Even the most senior salesman back in Seattle hadn't made half what these people did. She would need to do more research on wages in this area before she put out any help wanted ads.

She put the cup back on the tray and got ready for bed. Tomorrow would be soon enough to worry.

* * * *

The next morning, Cayce went to the lobby for a local newspaper. Spreading the paper out on the bed, she focused on the ads in the back. From what she could tell, salaries here were in line with what she'd expect to pay in a big city. Cheaper than Seattle, but not what Matthew had been shelling out. She folded the paper and put it into her tote. Time to get to work!

This time, the shop's door was locked when she arrived. Sarah had been told to stay home. Cayce pushed the door open and re-locked it, noticing the same homeless man standing across the street, watching her. With a friendly wave, she made her way back to the office with the Queen Anne desk. Working in Mr. Goldstein's office was impossible—the lingering smell from the blood-soaked rug turned her stomach. First project, inventory. She printed off the list she'd been given and found a clipboard in the desk. Then she went to the top floor of the building. She wanted to check out the apartment before she dug into inventory work.

By noon, she'd cleared only one floor. She'd spent longer in the apartment than she'd expected. The inventory was proving to be a problem. Several items that were listed as being on a particular floor were missing. Probably just moved, but where? She had no clue. Understanding the inventory was going to take longer than she'd planned.

Stopping at the break room, she grabbed a bottle of water. A noise from the hallway startled her. She held the bottle out like a weapon and made her way to her office. Nic sat at her desk, eating a sandwich and playing on his phone. She took a deep breath, trying to calm her nerves. "How did you get in?"

"You left the door open." He nodded to the Styrofoam container. "Eat. I brought you lunch."

"I didn't leave the door unlocked." She glanced down the hallway and heard laughter. "What's going on here? Harry?"

"I believe the building spirits are teasing you." Nic lifted his head listened for an answer from the unseen inhabitants. "Apparently, they unlocked the door to let me inside."

Cayce narrowed her eyes. "Are you sure you didn't take Sarah's keys?"

Nic took a set of keys out of his pocket and slid them across the desk. "Sleight of hand is a family tradition."

She examined the lunch. Ham and cheese croissant and a small container of potato salad along with a bag of chips. Her stomach growled. When she had wolfed most of it down, she leaned back and asked, "Really, why are you here?"

"I've been doing some checking around about your business. Goldstein was circling the bankruptcy drain. Email your lawyer and have him get you out of the deal since the guy died before the three-day waiting period was over."

"I don't want out of the deal. I studied the books last night and from what I've seen, the financial crisis is solvable. The sales are here. His expenses were just too high." She opened the bag of chips.

"Like what?" He threw his lunch into a plastic trash bag. "It couldn't be from the cleaning staff."

"Let's just say Mr. Goldstein's employees must have loved working here." She grabbed the notebook from her bag. "Do you know an Arnold Barnett?"

"No, should I?" He put his empty lunch container in a plastic bag.

"Just wondering. I'm going over to his place now. Since Matthew didn't tell anyone about the sale, I feel like I should reach out to his employees. Especially ones that meant so much that Goldstein overpaid them." Cayce opened the notebook where she'd noted Arnold Barnett's address. "It's just down the street. According to the schedule, he works weekends. I need to tell him he's unemployed."

"Mind if I tag along?" He swept her lunch receptacle into the trash sack. "Dumpster in the back?"

After showing Nic the dumpster in the alley, they walked two blocks farther into the French Quarter, then turned left down a one-way street. Nic leaned close and glanced behind them, whispering, "We're being followed."

"I know. It's the homeless guy who sleeps outside the shop. He's been following us since we left." Cayce didn't turn back since she could see the guy's reflection in the window of the restaurant as they walked past. "I think he's harmless."

"I'll tell the police that when they're investigating your murder in that rat trap of a building." Nic pointed to an iron gate. "This is the address."

They stepped into an entryway that led to an interior courtyard where a fountain bubbled over a moss-covered statue. Sarah Stiner sat crying near the fountain. When she heard their footsteps, she stood and hurried past them without a word.

"Hey, Sarah. What are you doing here?" Cayce started to go after her but stopped at the entry. Then she came back to the bottom of the stairs. "I seem to have this effect on people."

Nic nodded to the stairwell. "One problem at a time. Let's see why she was here."

They climbed the narrow stairway and went down the walk to the door marked 201. When she knocked, the door was thrown open revealing a small living room furnished in priceless antiques. Cayce stared at a lion bust and the polished foyer table it sat on. She glanced around the room ticking items off her inventory list.

"Sarah, I told you to leave me alone. It's not my fault you didn't take care of your own future." A small man in a Nike T-shirt with a gray scruff of beard finally looked up from his phone. "Oh, sorry, I thought you were—"

"I saw Sarah in the foyer. Why was she here?" The more he said before he realized who she was, the better.

Arnold Barnett ran a hand through his thinning hair. "She's upset about what happened to our boss. I can't blame her. We worked together for over five years. We're more than just co-workers."

"Are you lovers?" Nic leaned against the doorway, looking way more casual than Cayce knew he felt.

"What? No! We were all friends." He paused. "I guess it doesn't matter now, but Sarah was in love with the boss. It was hard to watch, her being so head-over-heels and him, totally oblivious."

"So they weren't a couple? It was all one-sided?" Cayce watched the man's face for reactions.

"Who knows? I don't pry into people's business." He glanced back into the small living room. "Look, I'm job hunting, so unless you're here to tell me I'm one of the ones you're keeping on, I need to end this conversation."

"Glad you know who I am. It makes things faster." Cayce leaned to the left, trying to see more of the apartment. The rumor mill had been working hard if she was already recognized as the new owner of Goldstein's Antiques. "One question before I deliver the bad news. I've been going through the accounting. Can you tell me why you were being paid twice the salary that's normal for your position?"

A smile curved Arnold's lips. "You are into the details, aren't you?"

When Cayce didn't respond, Arnold shrugged. "What can I say, Matthew was generous to a fault. And I'm really, really good at what I do."

Exasperated, Cayce knew she wouldn't get any more out of him. She needed to call Detective Charles and get her property back. She turned to Nic. "Let's go. There's nothing here."

"What's that supposed to mean?" Arnold curled his fist.

Nic stepped in between Cayce and Arnold. "I don't think you want to do that."

Cayce could almost see the wheels moving in Arnold's head before he dropped his arm and uncurled his fingers. He grabbed the door. "Just leave. There's nothing more I want to say to you."

As they made their way out to the street, neither Cayce nor Nic spoke until they had turned the corner. "He's hiding something," Nic mumbled.

"You mean beside the fact that several of my missing antiques are in his apartment?" Cayce paused a minute and grabbed her notebook. "Let me write down what I saw so I can check it against the inventory list."

Nic paced on the sidewalk, waiting for her to finish. "I don't believe Sarah was just there to grieve. She's part of this."

Cayce tucked the notebook back into her tote. "You think she killed Matthew? Or that Sarah and Arnold killed him?"

"I think either one is a good bet. Of course, there's no proof." Nic sighed and leaned up against the wall with Cayce. "I'm not feeling good about this. I would really like you to come stay at the compound."

"That's not going to happen." Cayce didn't like the fact they were still having this argument.

A voice interrupted their fight. "Check the video."

It was the homeless man standing by the corner, watching them. "Did you say something?"

"Mr. Goldstein installed cameras. He knew there was something wrong with the store. He hired me to watch at night, but I didn't see anything." The man shook his head. "I must have fallen asleep. Stupid, stupid."

"There are cameras in the store?" Cayce took a step toward the guy, but he ran out into traffic.

"Stupid me, stupid me," he chanted. Car horns blared as he darted between two cars.

Cayce stared after him. She started powerwalking toward the shop. "Let's go find these cameras."

It took them a while to find the closet where Matthew Goldstein had set up a security system. Four monitors showed the main showroom, the outside, the back door, and Matthew's office. Nic glanced at the system. "I don't want to mess with this. Call your detective friend."

Later that day, Detective Charles sat in Cayce's office. "He hit him with one of those statue things. While his back was turned. What a coward."

"While you were watching the videos, I matched the list of everything that was supposed to be in inventory that I saw in Barnett's apartment." She handed him the list. "Arnold Barnett didn't just kill Matthew; he was stealing from him. All of these items should be at the shop."

"We'll let you go through the apartment as soon as the crime scene guys get done with it. It might take a while for you to get everything back, but at least you'll have a full list." He nodded to the coffeepot. "Mind if I have a cup? I think it's going to be a long night."

"Have a seat, I'll get it. Black?" Cayce nodded to the other visitor chair.

"Perfect. Besides the evidence you gathered, I got a call from the station a few minutes ago. Sarah Stiner came in and confessed to cooking the books. Arnold Barnett told her he was going to kill the old man, but she didn't believe him. Until it happened."

"I don't understand—why would she confess?" Cayce asked the detective as sipped his coffee.

"She said Harry told her she had to if she wanted to sleep at night." The detective sat down his cup as Nic and Cayce exchanged glances. "So, who's Harry?"

KEEPSAKES

J.A. CHALKLEY

Thunder rumbled in the distance as Lynn Weber hurried up the steps and across the portico to a set of massive double doors. Large white columns coupled with ivy-covered walls gave the mansion an air of Old South charm.

Lynn half expected Scarlett O'Hara to throw open the doors and greet her with a glass of lemonade. She had no doubt that the brass lion-head door knockers staring down at her were worth more than her car. As tempting as they were, she reached to use the doorbell instead. Beyond the doors, bells chimed her arrival with a piece of classical music she vaguely remembered from a Saturday morning cartoon.

Lightening flashed, causing the hair on her arms to tingle. She eased closer to the door, counting off the distance until thunder marked the storm's approach. Two and a half, it was moving fast. Receiving no response to the doorbell, she reached for the ring hanging from one of the lion's jaws. It moved out of her grasp as the door swung open.

Before she stood, a small woman with dark eyes that glared out from hawkish features that seemed frozen in a scowl. Her floral perfume hit Lynn with enough force to take her breath away. "Miss Weber?"

Definitely, not Scarlett. "Yes." Lynn managed to choke out. "You must be, Ann Harper, Mrs. Anderson's assistant. We spoke on the phone." Lynn held out a hand. It was ignored.

"You're late." Ann Harper stepped back holding the door open for her. The woman looked like a matron from an old forties prison movie, complete with a ring of keys jangling from the belt at her waist.

"Sorry." Certain any excuse would be rejected Lynn offered none. Once she was clear of the threshold, the heavy door closed with a sharp click. It sent a shudder down her spine.

"Follow me. Please." It was clear the *please* had been tacked on as an afterthought. Not waiting for an answer, Ann spun on the heels of her sensible shoes, and stalked away.

Lynn hurried to catch up. They entered a dark, wood-paneled study. Paintings, framed newspaper articles, and accolades lined the walls. Overstuffed leather chairs and expensive rugs were scattered about. The room reeked of old money.

"Wait here. Mrs. Anderson will be with you shortly." She waited till Lynn had perched in the offered chair before disappearing through the door.

Releasing a shaky breath, Lynn settled back in the leather chair, only to freeze as a loud noise that could be mistaken for something other than uncomfortable furniture squeaked in the quiet room. Heat flushed her cheeks at the sound.

Her attention was drawn to a large oil painting hanging over the stone fireplace. Katherine Anderson stared back at her. Judging by her blond hair and smooth skin, Lynn guessed the woman to be in her mid-to-late twenties. She did a quick calculation—the painting had to be over fifty years old. There was nothing more recent in the room. A hint of a smile on the woman's lips offset the portrait's formality. It made her seem impish. Maybe it was one of the reasons she'd snagged three rich husbands over the last six decades. *And managed to outlive them all.*

Lynn slipped a hand into her backpack, tracing fingertips over a manila envelope. For the hundredth time she wondered if she should have gone to the police first with her suspicions. *And give up my chance to break the story? No. This is my baby, and nobody is going to steal it out from under me.*

Ignoring the chair's protests, she pulled out her phone. With a quick check to assure she was alone, she snapped several photos of the room. They might come in handy for reference later—at least, that was the story she was sticking to.

Portraits of old men in three-piece suits lined one wall. Three she recognized as Katherine's deceased husbands. She had no idea who the others were.

Outside the wind began to pick up, causing the shrubs to tap against the window glass. Lynn's attention turned to the desk. Various trinkets and an expensive pen set made it look more like a store display than a working desk. She snapped another photo.

Her gaze settled on a glass-dome display of a well-worn wristwatch. The leather band had seen better days, and the face bore small scratches. Lynn was no expert, but it looked vaguely military, maybe from the thirties or forties. Closer inspection revealed a Marine Corps emblem on the leather. There was something familiar about the watch. Whatever it was danced at the back of her mind, just out of reach. Beside the watch sat another display case, this one square and empty. There was no clue as to what it once held. She snapped pictures of both.

Satisfied, she pulled up her story notes. After two years of intense research she knew the material by heart. Still, it couldn't hurt to check them once more. A newspaper article popped up.

Missing Sutherland Girl Found in Shallow Grave at Lake Chesdin.

The bold headline took up most of the front page. Dated April 14, 1970, the story touched on brief details of the girl's disappearance two years earlier. Nearly fifty years had passed, but Paige Louise Archer would forever be the seventeen-year-old girl, beaming an angelic smile at the yearbook photographer. Hiding behind that smile, Lynn knew Paige had been a little hellion who had done things that would have made a sailor blush. None of which justified her being beaten to death and abandoned in an unmarked grave.

She paused at the sound of raised voices. Lightening brightened the room, followed a heartbeat later by thunder. By the time it had faded away, the voices were silent.

I'm letting this place get to me.

Lynn shook herself. Another swipe brought up a second article one dated May 10, 1971. *Local Brothers Drown During Fishing Tournament.* Beneath the headline was a grainy black and white photo of two men with their arms around each other's shoulders, each holding a large trout.

The caption below the photo read: Judge Robert Samuels (left) and Sheriff James Samuels, brothers celebrate after logging the largest catches for the first day of the Lake Chesdin 1971 Fishing Tournament. Both men sported well-developed beer guts, though Robert did a better job of hiding his. James looked like he'd pulled a weekend bender. There was a glassy eyed stare even the poor-quality photo couldn't hide.

Lynn had no doubt that he reeked of beer, unfiltered cigarettes, and sweat. And fish, she couldn't forget the fish smell. She shuttered at the thought. The photo had been taken two days before the brothers' boat went over the Lake Chesdin dam, drowning both. *Bet they were passed out drunk when it happened.*

Lightning bathed the room in white light; thunder rattled the window panels. Lynn jumped, silently cursing her jumpy nerves.

"Storms out here tend to be worse, as they follow the river." Katherine Anderson glided across the floor to stand before Lynn. She offered a hand. "Welcome to my humble abode, Miss Weber." Each word was enunciated with a precision learned in one of the South's finer boarding schools.

Lynn stood, taking the offered hand. It was ice cold. She could feel every bone beneath the paper-thin skin. She managed a smile, holding the old woman's gaze. Dark circles framed the dull, sunken eyes staring back at her. The woman was a ghost of the one in the painting.

"Thank you for accepting my request for an interview, Mrs. Anderson." Lynn ducked her head with a light chuckle. "I'd started to think you were going to ignore me."

The icy hand tightened with surprising strength. Lynn bit back a yelp, then she was free. Rain beat against the large windows.

Sunken eyes narrowed as they bore into Lynn's. "I had considered declining your request. But fate seems to be on your side in this matter. Besides, it's a perfect night for chasing ghosts." She gestured toward one of the windows as she moved behind the desk.

From a pocket she pulled out a small cloth. She reached over and opened the lid on the empty display box. With great care she unwrapped a worn gold coin and placed it atop the acrylic stand. "An old family keepsake. It's been handed down from mother to daughter for generations." She snapped the lid closed. "Legend has it, one of my great grandmothers stole it from a leprechaun."

"Really?" Lynn leaned forward for a closer look. The face of the coin showed a woman wearing a toga-style dress that covered one shoulder and breast. She held a sword across her lap and an olive branch in her other hand. Runic characters circled the figure. On the reverse of the coin, two crossed swords hung over the fallen body of a man. "It's very... unique."

"Yes, it is." Katherine settled into the leather wing backed chair, draping her hands over the armrests. Lynn couldn't shake the thought she looked like a queen holding court. "I understand you're researching the Paige Archer murder for a book."

"Yes. It started as my college research project and became a bit of an obsession."

"Obsessions can be dangerous things, Miss Weber."

The sunken eyes bored through her. For a fleeting moment, she considered bolting for her car and not looking back. Instead she smiled, holding up the phone. "Yes, they can. Do you mind if I record this?"

Katherine eyed the phone. "I'd rather you didn't."

"Okay. No problem." Lynn shoved the phone into her backpack and pulled out a notebook and pen. "Sometimes old school is better."

Katherine didn't laugh.

"All right then." Lynn leaned forward in the chair, gritting her teeth against the awkward squeal of the leather.

Ann Harper appeared in the doorway with a tray. She set it clumsily on the desk, causing the china to rattle. "It's time for your pill, ma'am." Not waiting for an answer, she poured a cup of tea, lightened it with milk and a sugar cube, and handed it to Katherine.

"Thank you, Ann. Please, pour for Miss Weber, then you may leave us."

Lynn couldn't see Ann's face, but she caught the raised eyebrow Katherine shot the woman.

"One lump or two," Ann growled as she turned to Lynn.

"Two, please." Lynn smiled.

It was not returned as two sugar cubes plopped into the tea before the cup and saucer were thrust at Lynn.

She tucked the notebook under one arm to balance the fine china in both hands. "Thank you."

Without a word, Ann turned and left the room.

Lynn leaned forward to whisper. "Have I offended her?"

"She's just pouting." Katherine waved a hand toward the empty doorway. "It'll pass."

"How long has she been working for you?"

"It seems like a lifetime." Katherine picked up the pill from the serving tray. "Cancer." She placed the pill in her mouth and washed it down with the tea.

"Excuse me?"

"The pill is for my cancer."

"Oh, I'm sorry."

"It's not the demise I would have chosen, but there's still time to choose another."

Unsure if she was meant to reply, Lynn chose to remain silent.

"Why do you want to solve this case, Miss Weber?"

"I'd like to give Paige Archer the justice she deserves."

"People seldom get what they deserve." She lifted her cup and took a sip.

Something in her tone made Lynn's skin crawl. "Someone murdered a pregnant teenage girl. They need to be brought to justice."

"Justice?" Katherine chuckled. The sound added to Lynn's anxiety. "Justice isn't always delivered in a courtroom. Sometimes fate serves it up in more satisfying ways."

"Did you serve *justice* to Paige Archer?"

A delicate eyebrow arched at the question. Katherine lowered her cup. "Are you accusing me of Paige Archer's murder?"

"You had a motive."

"Do tell." She raised the cup.

"She was pregnant with your husband's baby."

"I hope you have proof to back up such slander." Katherine took a sip of tea.

"I do." Lynn sat her cup on the desk. She pulled the envelope from her backpack and held it out.

Katherine eyed it a moment. Her gaze shifted to Lynn as she sat aside the teacup and took the envelope. Long fingernails slipped under the flap popping it open. She pulled out several photos.

Lynn felt a twinge of smug satisfaction as the old woman's cool façade cracked.

She placed the photos back in the envelope without looking through them. "Where did you get these?"

"They were in a box of Paige's belongings. Her aunt inherited it after Paige's parents passed away. The photos, along with her diary were in it."

"Diary? The police searched every inch of the Archer house for her diary."

"The diary, along with the photos, was hidden in a secret compartment in the bottom of her jewelry box. I guess no one bothered to look there."

Katherine chuckled. "No, James never would have thought of that."

"James? You mean, Sheriff Anderson?"

"Yes, he took over the investigation after Deputy Milton's death." Katherine tossed the envelope onto the desk and settled back in her chair. "I still don't see how this makes me a murderer."

"Paige described her affair with Robert in detail. She was going to confront you about the affair. And the baby."

"And?"

"And that was her last entry. She disappeared the next day. After Paige's body was found, your husband paid for her funeral. According to Paige's aunt, he insisted the bodies be cremated. Nice way to avoid any further testing. Any evidence with possible DNA samples is missing from the case file, along with several pages of investigation notes. It would have been easy for a Sheriff to make such things *disappear*."

Thin lips curled back over perfect teeth. Lynn couldn't shake the feeling she was a mouse at the mercy of a cat. "*I* offered to pay for Paige's funeral. My husband, the Judge, insisted it be a cremation, not to destroy evidence, but because he was cheap. He liked to play the saint, but always on a budget."

"Did Paige confront you about the affair?"

Lightning and thunder struck at the same moment, shaking the house. The lights flickered before abandoning the room to darkness. Lynn's heart began to race. She yelped as a lighter flared, shadowing the sharp features of Ann Harper. Ignoring Lynn's outburst, she placed the flame to a candle sitting on the desk. Its shadows danced about the room.

"You said the repairman fixed that generator," Katherine snipped.

"I told you not to pay him up front," Ann replied. She turned and walked away, missing the glare Katherine shot at her back. Katherine mumbled something under her breath Lynn couldn't make out. "I heard that." Ann called from the hallway.

"I'm sure you did, with those bat ears of yours." Satisfied with the last word Katherine settled back into her chair. "Now where were we?"

"Did Paige come to you about the affair?"

"Yes, she came here, all full of piss and vinegar. Sat in that very chair." A bony finger pointed at Lynn. "Announced that she was having Robert's baby, and I should start packing, as she was going to be the new Mrs. Robert Samuels."

"What did you do?"

"I laughed and told her the Judge would do what he always did in these situations. He'd put her on a bus to Charlottesville with some money and the address of a doctor who would fix the problem."

"So, this wasn't his first affair?"

"Hardly." Katherine chuckled, shaking her head.

"You never thought about killing Paige?"

"Oh, I thought about it, but fate was on her side that day. I tried to tell the Judge that, but he wouldn't listen. He never believed in fate. That's why it turned against him."

"Did your husband kill Paige?"

Katherine looked her square in the eye. "The Judge never did his own dirty work."

"Are you saying he had someone else kill her? Who?" She paused. "It was James, wasn't it?"

"You're smarter than I gave you credit for Miss Weber."

"How can you be certain it was James and not Robert?"

"Because Robert would never have trusted anyone else to do it. Their brotherly bond was strong. Besides, James would have enjoyed it. From the day he took his first step, he liked to hurt things. Insects, puppies, his wife. Once he was elected sheriff, there were no limits to his cruelty."

"When did you start to suspect Robert had her killed?"

"From day one. But it was several months before I learned the truth. One day Deputy Milton came to speak with me. He'd found evidence of the affair and suspected Robert and James were involved in Paige's death."

"There's nothing in his case notes about it." Lynn said.

"After his death, James went through the case file and purged anything that might point to Robert."

"James told you this?"

"I watched him hand the notes to Robert. He burned them in the fireplace." Her eyes shifted to the stone mantel. "The same place where James murdered Ollie Milton."

"Excuse me? Deputy Milton died in a car crash."

"No, James beat him to death with a fireplace poker, then staged the car crash as a cover."

"You witnessed this?"

"Yes, it was quite brutal." She reached for the teacup. "Ruined one of my favorite rugs."

Lynn's mouth dropped into a shocked O. "Why didn't you go to the authorities?"

"Robert and James *were* the authorities, dear. I would have suffered one of James' *accidents* long before I could have testified. Besides, their fates hadn't been decided yet." She sipped at her tea.

Lynn's mind spun as the pieces began to come together. Her gaze fell on the watch display, and another piece snapped into place. "Had their fates been decided when you drowned them in the river?"

The teacup paused midway to Katherine's lips. She didn't look up. "First you accuse me of murdering my husband's mistress and now my husband. Before you ask, I can prove I wasn't in Dallas during the Kennedy assassination." A smirk crossed her lips as she took a sip.

"According to the report on your husband's death, the last time you saw him was the day he left for the fishing tournament, three days before he drowned."

"That's correct."

"Then how did his watch end up on your desk?"

"That's not his watch." There was a chill in the answer. "It belonged to my grandfather."

"Then why was Robert wearing it in all the photos with Paige?" Lynn pulled out her phone and swiped through several screens. "And during the fishing tournament two days before he died." She held up the newspaper article with the grainy photo.

Katherine didn't look at it. "It was given to me with his personal affects."

"No, I've read the report, there is no mention of a watch in his belongings. You took it off him before you sent his boat over the dam."

Jaw muscles worked beneath pale skin. "The Judge had a habit of taking things he liked. He took a fancy to my grandfather's watch. So, I took it back."

"Before or after you murdered him?"

"Murder is such a nasty word. I saw it more as self-preservation. The Samuel brothers were a dangerous duo. They had come to see murder as an acceptable solution to their problems. I knew it was only a matter of time before I would be a problem for them to solve."

"You're claiming self-defense?"

"As I said, self-preservation." She took another sip of tea.

"You know I have to report this to the authorities?"

"I'm dying, Miss Weber. Your justice will have to move swiftly if it wishes to catch me."

"How did you do it?"

"Horse tranquilizers in the prepared meals I sent with them. I knew which night they would eat them, so I slipped up to the cabin and waited in the woods. They were out cold when the boat went over the dam."

"There is no way you could have carried them to the boat by yourself. Who helped you?"

"My sins are my own to confess. If others wish to unburden their souls, I'll not deprive them of the chance." Across the room a grandfather clock began to chime the hour. "I've given you all my secrets, Miss Weber. Do with them as you wish." Katherine set down her teacup. "It's getting late, and this trip down memory lane has drained me." She stood.

Lynn scrambled to her feet.

"Ann will show you out."

"Thank you for your time, Mrs. Anderson." Lynn thrust out her hand. "And your honesty."

Katherine eyed the offered hand a moment before taking it. Somehow her hand was colder than before. "Fate smiled on you this evening, Miss Weber. If you're lucky it will continue to do so."

"I hope so. If you like, I can send you a copy of the book once it's finished."

"That won't be necessary. I already know the ending. Besides, I won't be here to read it. Good evening, Miss Weber." Not waiting for a reply, she turned and disappeared into the darkness beyond the study door.

"This way."

Lynn jumped as Ann picked up the candle and started away. *How does she do that?* She hurried to catch up to the woman who was already standing by the open door. The storm had moved on, leaving behind a light rain.

Lynn stepped through the doorway and turned back. "Mrs. Harper, may I—" The door slammed. "I guess that's a no." Relieved to be free of the place, she hurried to her car.

* * * *

There was a sharp knock at the door. Lynn pressed *save* on her document before checking the peephole. She startled at the figure standing in the hallway of her apartment. Her hand hovered over the lock a moment before clicking it open. "Mrs. Harper, what are you doing here?"

"Mrs. Anderson is dead. She passed away in her sleep last night."

"I... I'm sorry to hear that." Caught off guard by the abrupt announcement, Lynn brushed at her hair, trying to think of a better response.

"She wanted you to have this."

Lynn eyed the small display case resting in the woman's outstretched hand. Light reflected off the gold coin's surface. "Why would she give it to me?"

"She didn't. Fate chose you."

"Okay... thanks." Lynn took the box. "With her gone, what will you do?"

"I'm moving to Fiji, so I can sit on the beach while Cabana boys bring me frozen drinks."

Lynn ducked her head unable to hide a smile. "Good for you."

"Yes, it will be." Ann turned to leave. She paused. "I'm glad you won the coin toss."

"What coin toss?"

"The one the night of your visit. Katherine felt we should let Fate decide your destiny."

"You tossed to see if she would speak with me?"

"No, we tossed to decide if we should kill you or not."

"Ki... Kill me?"

"Yes, but Fate smiled on you that evening." Ann's sharp features softened into something that could pass for a smile. It only made her more terrifying.

"Fate?" Lynn's mind struggled to process the revelation.

"Yes, the coin." Ann tapped a fingernail against the box. "That's its name, Fate. Trust Fate, and it will never lead you astray. Goodbye, Miss Weber."

Lynn slammed the door shut, clicking the deadbolt into place. She leaned against the door with a heavy sigh and held up the coin. "Well, Fate, I guess I owe you one."

SOUTHERN SISTERS STICK TOGETHER

STACIE GILES

"You're a sight for sore eyes." Vera smiled at hearing her cousin call to her from the sidewalk. Her long dark skirt swished as she closed the front door of the Memphis YWCA where she lived and turned toward him.

"Good morning, Burnell. Are you just off work? You look like you need your bed." Burnell had recently begun working for the police department and was stuck on night shift.

"I hoped you'd be happier to see me than that." He pretended to pout as he followed Vera along the Madison Street sidewalk.

"Always happy to see you, but I'm on my way to work and Mrs. Florence won't put up with late waitresses at Gerber's Tea Room. I'm still in my probationary period, remember?" Still, Vera slowed her pace and peered closely at her cousin. Growing up on neighboring family farms a long way from Memphis, they were as close as brother and sister, and she realized he was worried. "Is something on your mind, Burnell?"

She knew both their families had charged him with watching out for her in the big city. It had been wonderful to have him show her around her first few days in Memphis and help her settle into a rented room at the YWCA, but she didn't want a Nosey Parker watching her every move. After all, it was 1920, the start of a new decade. Just last week, Tennessee had ratified the 19th Amendment finally giving women the right to vote. She set her lips in a firm line.

Burnell sighed and looked grave. "Come on—it's just nine blocks to Gerber's. I'll tell you on the way." They were nearly to Main Street before he began, and Vera let him take his time. "Last night a young lady was found in an alley behind the William Len Hotel. It was real late and no one else was around. At first, the policeman on the beat thought it was a drunk passed out. But then he saw it was a woman, dressed in real nice clothes, a lady. Not what you usually see down around South Main. She didn't smell boozy, but she wouldn't wake up, and she looked like there'd, um, been some trouble."

Vera's brow creased. A disturbing story, but why had Burnell come to tell it to her? He hadn't been with the police but a few months; still, he must have seen disturbing things before this.

Burnell sighed again, more deeply. "The officer got some help, and they brought her in, had the doctor look her over. She'll be all right, but she was, um, assaulted." His head bowed slightly, then came back up. "Not robbed, though. Still had her jewelry, and they found her handbag nearby, but she can't remember a thing." Burnell looked Vera in the eye. "The doctor thinks someone gave her knockout drops. Do you know about them?"

"You mean it wasn't just some bad hooch?" Vera queried. "I know Boss Crump doesn't enforce Prohibition here in Memphis, but it *does* mean the liquor is mostly home brew, even in nice restaurants like the one in that hotel."

"No, and that's what scares me. She thought she was just going out to dinner with a decent man, then woke up being carried into the police station. She's so embarrassed; she won't say a thing about who she was with. Says she can't believe he would do anything wrong. Mostly I think she's just afraid talk will get out—you know she'd never live it down. We may be 'modern' now, but no young girl wants something like that getting out about her, whether she's a 'flapper' or not."

"She won't tell you who did this to her?" Vera gasped.

"No, she won't, and we can't make her. Anyway, we could never prove he drugged her or, well, anything else. I don't blame her for keeping it to herself, but I'm afraid this piker, whoever he is, will do it again. That's why I'm telling you." Burnell turned to face her, his eyes deadly serious, and reached out to take her arm. "You've got to know how these drops work. They're clear liquid, so you can't see them, and it doesn't take much to make you woozy. The doctor said they have kind of a bitter taste, but it's pretty easy to cover up. Seems their effect is unpredictable—what would make one person sick to their stomach might make another one lose consciousness or even kill them."

As they approached the employee entrance to the department store, Burnell took a newspaper from under his arm and held it out to Vera. "Look here, I don't want you saying anything about this to anybody. The girl's not talking and it would only make trouble for her." He sighed yet again. "But I brought you this newspaper with an article about knockout drops so you can share it with the other girls and warn them. The doctor had a few copies and he handed them out, told us that even if we couldn't tell about the girl last night, we could still warn the womenfolk."

Vera's eyes were drawn to the lurid headline: *Dangerous KO Drops Found in Chicago, NY, Memphis*, on the front page of the Chattanooga newspaper. "Two girls in Chicago were assaulted, robbed, and murdered by some men using these knockout drops," Burnell said, summarizing the article. "And a man in New York was robbed after someone put the drops in his drink. Doesn't remember a thing, even though he walked for blocks before he collapsed." Burnell shook his head and looked directly at Vera. "And it's not just up North—seems the State Pharmacy Inspector got a tip, so he has come to Memphis to check out all the pharmacies." He paused, shaking his head.

"Burnell, I've got to be in uniform by eight," Vera pleaded, worried about her job.

"Okay, okay, but be careful. The inspector has found plenty of problems. He's fined some pharmacies and even made arrests. But he's still looking for some missing chloral hydrate—knockout drops—so you and your friends need to watch out for anything suspicious." He turned agonized eyes on Vera. "Go on, now. I'll be here to see you home when the Tea Room closes at 5:00." He thrust the paper at her and walked quickly southward down the alley toward Front Street and his boarding house.

Vera dashed down the stairs into the cellar locker room and hurriedly changed into a dark shirtwaist that matched her skirt. It struck her that her shift didn't end until 6:00 when cleanup was done, but there was no way now to tell Burnell. "Oh well," she thought, "he'll just have to wait in the store." As she attached her white collar and cuffs, she considered how to share news of the knockout drops with the others.

After she'd put on her white cap and apron, the girl at the locker next to her asked, "Vera, check me over, will you?"

"Just right, Ellen. Do the same for me?" Ellen fastened Vera's hairpins, and they joined the other waitresses climbing the back stairs to the kitchen of the 5th floor Tea Room to report at 8:00 sharp. It wouldn't open until 10:00, but the girls would be busy setting tables, folding napkins, arranging flowers, and handling the many other delicate touches that made Gerber's Tea Room the favorite gathering place of Memphis society. Vera shot Ellen a concerned glance when they saw the new bob haircut on Louise, one of the older, more experienced girls. "I hope Mrs. Florence doesn't fire her," whispered Ellen.

Vera barely managed to secrete Burnell's newspaper behind a stack of plates before Mrs. Florence stepped up to inspect them all. The manager's compressed lips telegraphed her displeasure with the new haircut, but all she said to Louise was, "Meet me in my office after your shift."

Poor girl, she'll be out of a job by the end of the day, thought Vera. Everyone knew Mrs. Florence insisted that "her girls" present a traditional model of decorum. Vera was grateful that the job was teaching her about city manners, dress, and society's expectations. It was a great chance for a girl straight off the farm. She might have made more working in a cotton mill, but $8 a week to start plus meals and tips was nothing to sneeze at.

Preparations for opening kept Vera too busy to do anything with Burnell's newspaper. She concentrated on lining up napkins, silverware, and glasses just so, making sure the linen was spotless, putting carefully arranged fresh flowers in tiny vases on every table, and precisely placing portions of desserts on doily-lined china, ready to be served. A few women were waiting to enter at opening time, and patrons poured in until past the lunch hour. Her assigned tables were in the back, the last to be filled, but Vera kept busy in the kitchen when she wasn't serving customers.

It was nearly 2:00 before she had a chance to retrieve the newspaper from its hiding place. She had decided to simply give the article to Mrs. Florence when Louise saw it in her hand and drawled, "What you got there, sugar? Not busy enough?" She snatched the paper from Vera, adding, "Why don't you take over those two women at Table Eight? It looks like they'll never leave." Vera understood, since she had quickly learned that women patrons were often much more demanding, kept their seats longer, and tipped less than men. She didn't much care for Louise, but didn't want to antagonize the pretty, willful girl who was admired by many of the other waitresses for her boldness and daring. She started to acquiesce when it occurred to her that Louise might be the solution she needed. The girls would listen to a warning about knockout drops from the worldly Louise much more readily than from herself or Mrs. Florence.

"Sure, I'll take Table Eight, if you like." Vera said nonchalantly. She nodded at the newspaper, now in Louise's grip. "Look at what it says about knockout drops. There is chloral hydrate missing right here in Memphis. Anybody could drop some in what we're drinking without us even knowing. We girls have to watch out for each other."

Vera smiled, satisfied to see the other waitresses in the kitchen crowd around Louise, who began reading the article aloud. Out in the Tea Room, Vera was pleased by the appreciative smiles from the women at Table Eight when she brought them a fresh pot of tea along with their desserts. She returned to the kitchen, shaking her head at Louise's attitude toward female customers, and was dismayed to hear Louise dismissing the newspaper article.

"What are they trying to say, that we should all run and hide just because some old pharmacists can't keep their inventory straight? I'll bet those girls in Chicago were no better than they should have been, and that's how they ended up murdered. And that man in New York probably just didn't want to tell his wife where he'd spent all his money," Louise guffawed and looked pointedly at the girls around her until they joined in her laughter. She smiled in satisfaction, "Scare tactics, trying to keep us in our place. But we can take care of ourselves, right, girls?"

Disappointed, Vera seized a dishcloth and began wiping the table where the desserts were lined up. "Burnell would never make up a story like he told me. I wish I could tell them what happened last night," she thought, frustrated. Ellen came up next to her and started laying doilies on china dessert plates, preparing for the usual rush of customers from 3:00 until closing at 5:00. Men came more frequently in the afternoon and the cook would be kept busy filling their orders, which tended to be much heavier and require more cooking than the omelets, chicken salad sandwiches, and soups that women favored.

"I was thinking about those knockout drops," Ellen whispered. "Do you know much about them?" Vera shook her head and responded just as quietly. "Just that they have no color, taste a little bitter but not real strong, and people react differently to them, from getting sick to being totally knocked out." Vera waited for Ellen to say more, but she seemed to drop the subject and instead started talking about how she'd spent the previous weekend.

"Last Sunday, Sarah asked me to go to the Fair with her and a man she met working at the Old Tea Shop, you know, the one on Monroe Street near the Medical Center. Lots of men go there, so she does pretty well with tips, but she says you have to learn how to not let anybody get too fresh. She's a real good girl, and I think she manages her customers pretty well."

Ellen continued, "One man was friendly to her—in a nice way—and when he invited her to visit the Fairground, she said she wanted to bring me along. He was respectable, name of Albert, a new doctor at the Medical Center. At first, it seemed all right. He picked us up at our boarding house in his Model T—it was fun to drive all the way to the Fairground in that," Ellen smiled, but then got quiet and looked down at her shoes.

Vera prompted her, "But it wasn't all right?"

Ellen wrinkled her nose as she answered. "Well, I can't put my finger on it, but he seemed a little strange. For one thing, he bought us all sodas, and insisted we drink them. I didn't want mine—soda makes me burp, but I couldn't tell him that, so I just said I wasn't thirsty. He wouldn't stop teasing me for being persnickety, so I finally took it. I took a drink, but I didn't like how it tasted, so I poured most of it out on the grass while he was talking with Sarah. I don't think he saw me, but after that he kept looking at me funny. Sarah drank hers up, because he told her to. Pretty soon, I said we had to go, but he kept trying to keep us at the Fairgrounds. I could see, though, that Sarah wasn't feeling too well, so I finally got us home."

"Did you have to find your own way home?" Vera was appalled to think the man had left Ellen and Sarah to get themselves home alone after dark.

"Oh, no, he was a perfect gentleman as far as that goes, drove us to the door. But Sarah was *not* well. I put her right to bed when we got home. I just felt like something was strange, you know, the way I had to keep insisting that we needed to leave?"

Mrs. Florence came into the kitchen through the swinging doors and admonished, "Girls, keep a watch out for patrons at your tables. The rush will start soon, and we don't want to keep anyone waiting."

Vera and Ellen glanced meaningfully at each other as they returned their attention to waitressing. Patrons soon filled the tables, and Vera was too busy to think about Ellen's story. She was on her way to give the cook an order when she heard a loud CRASH! reverberate through the Tea Room. Looking back at her tables, she saw Ellen frozen upright with a pile of dirty china and utensils on the floor in front of her. Vera seized a rag and rushed to her side. Smiling reassuringly, she took the tray from Ellen's hand and bent down to start piling dishes on it.

Ellen knelt beside her and started wiping the floor. "He pinched me!" she whispered, furious.

Vera carefully avoided looking at the two men at the table behind them as she worked, but her ears pricked up when one said to the other, "I've worked out most of the issues, but the Dean thought you might be able to help me solve the problem with the chloral hydrate."

With Mrs. Florence's eye upon them, Vera and Ellen carried the tray with its collection of broken dishes and the dirty rags back to the kitchen, eyes modestly cast down. Once inside the swinging doors, Ellen hissed, "It's him! It's Albert, from last weekend!"

Knowing that Mrs. Florence was watching them closely to see how they handled the cleanup, Vera nodded to Ellen, picked up two menus, and returned to the tea room.

As she approached the two men at the table, the dark-haired man looked directly at her and, with a slight motion of his head, indicated she should come to his side of the table rather than the side where she was headed. Unsure which of the two men was Albert the pincher, she ignored him. He repeated the action and, curious to see if he was doing this so he could pinch her, too, she decided to follow his lead. Drawing herself up stiffly, she moved to his side and proffered both menus to the dark-haired man, who took them and passed one to his blond companion.

"Aw, Glen," smirked the blond man, "are you trying to keep all the pretty girls for yourself?"

A small, satisfied sigh escaped Vera at Albert's self-revelation. "I'll be right back for your orders, gentlemen," she told them, then slipped behind the nearest pillar.

In just a few moments, she heard Albert say to Glen, "What makes you think I can help you find the missing chloral hydrate?"

Glen's reply was very dry. "Is it missing? I only told you I needed your help with an issue concerning it." Unable to stay in one place any longer, Vera returned to their table and asked for their order. As she was leaving, she heard Glen say, "As it happens, Albert, you're right, it *is* missing. Can you account for it?"

She took their order to the kitchen, where Louise seemed to be waiting for her. "Say, I could take that table of yours with the two guys right by the first pillar there," she said in an almost wheedling tone.

"No thanks, Louise," Vera answered, reluctant to put herself in debt to Louise. "I can manage."

Louise tossed her head, setting her bobbed hair swinging, and retorted, "Fine. Anyway, just so you know, that's *my* gentleman friend at that table. Albert. I'm seeing him tonight. He'll wait downstairs until I'm off, and then we're going to have a great time. I just thought I'd make it clear, that's all." She flounced through the swinging doors, letting them snap smartly.

Relieved at Louise's departure, Vera was nonetheless concerned for the older girl. Her thoughts raced. Louise was seeing Albert tonight. Albert was rude to women, as Ellen experienced last weekend and again today. The man named Glen was concerned about some chloral hydrate missing from the medical college pharmacy. He thought Albert had something to do with it. Ellen must have told her about the weekend episode with Albert because she suspected Albert of using knockout drops in their sodas. Albert isn't leaving Gerber's before meeting Louise, so he must be carrying the drops on him now, to use on her tonight. Louise isn't exactly my cup of tea, but I can't let her become the next victim. An impish grin replaced Vera's frown as a plan grew in her mind.

She took the men their meals, smiling at Glen when he again signaled her to come to his side of the table. His face lit up and his friendly brown eyes held hers a little longer than necessary. She tried to ignore the warmth she felt and concentrate instead on her plan. "I hope I don't lose my job because of this. But I probably will."

The crowd thinned as 5:00 approached, and Vera saw the hostess seat her cousin Burnell, already in his police uniform, close to her section. He had come as promised to walk her home. She was relieved to see him. He, at least, would understand what she was doing.

She approached Table Four beside the one where Glen and Albert sat, and picked up the family's nearly full teapot, promising to bring them a fresh one. Sidling between tables, she positioned herself right behind Albert. Suddenly she jerked forward, pretending to stumble and grabbing his chair to steady herself. The teapot she was carrying freely poured out warm tea, drenching his suit coat. He jumped up and pulled it off, swearing and gesticulating wildly.

Vera burst out with apologies as she deftly snatched up his coat. "Oh, I'm so sorry, sir. I'll take your coat right back into the kitchen and make sure it is as good as new by the time you're ready to go. I'll just leave your personal things here on the table." Moving quickly around the table toward Glen, she listed each item aloud as she removed it from the drenched coat's pockets and placed it on the table. "Here's your billfold, comb, watch and chain." She ignored Albert's splutters and shot a desperate look at Glen, who had also come to his feet. Glen responded to her look by moving closer to her, a questioning look on his face. "Here's your fountain pen, change purse, and, oh—what's this?" she asked, holding up a small glass bottle. "Chloral hydrate, the label says." She stepped behind Glen, who protectively fended off Albert as he lunged across the table at her.

Glen's jaw clenched as he grabbed Albert's arm and pulled it up behind the struggling man's back. "Dean Richards thought you might know where the chloral hydrate was. We'll head to his office right now." Glen's voice was low but intense enough to make it clear that Albert had no choice.

"Just a minute." Burnell quick-marched up to Albert. "We've been looking for a man in illegal possession of chloral hydrate. Let's all go down to the police station. We can call Dean Richards from there."

Relief washed over Vera as she handed the bottle to Burnell. He stored it safely in a pocket, then took control of Albert.

Vera was exhausted by the time she set out for the YWCA an hour later but remembering Mrs. Florence's words made her steps a little lighter. "That was very brave of you, Vera. Ellen told me what that awful man did to her friend, and I read that article you brought. Terrible! We women need to stick together!"

But the memory she hugged closest was of Glen when he was leaving the Tea Room behind Albert and Burnell. He stopped at the door and scanned the room, frowning, until he spotted Vera. Then he broke into a broad smile and tipped his hat to her before he turned and left. She took it as a promise.

THE POWER BEHIND THE THRONE

BARB GOFFMAN
Guest Author

"The defense calls Emily Forester."

My attorney squeezed my hand as I rose. If anyone noticed, they probably viewed it as a comforting gesture. I knew better. Bob was imploring me to follow his plan, not mine. *Too bad, Bob.* This was my murder trial, and we were doing things my way.

With my blond head held high and my lips pursed, I approached the witness stand. I had to look right. Innocent yet sad. It wasn't difficult. I truly was both of those things. I never meant to kill my husband. Well, not until he forced me to.

After being sworn in, I sat down, gliding my fingers over the bar at the front of the witness box. Its smooth, shiny wood reminded me how nice the floors in our main house had been when they'd been installed a few years ago. Clearly, it was time to refinish them, once I got this business out of the way.

Bob leaned forward from the counsel table. I wished he could have stood and approached the jury so they could fully take him in. Tall, dark-haired, with a granite chin, intelligent blue eyes, and a sharp charcoal suit, Bob was the type of man women noticed and men admired. Unfortunately, as I'd learned this week, North Carolina keeps its attorneys on a tight leash. Bob had to sit while he questioned me.

He smiled. "Please state your name for the record."

"Emily Forester."

"You're the wife of Aaron Forester?"

"Yes."

"Do you have any children?"

"Two." Now I smiled. "Seth is seventeen, and Lucy's sixteen."

"Where do you reside?"

I answered Bob's question about my home—both of my homes actually, the main house in Wake Forest and the beach house in nearby Sunset Beach, where Aaron had revealed his true colors.

Bob asked a few more preliminary questions before saying, "Can you please tell us what happened on August third of last year?"

I nodded. "I—"

"Objection!" The district attorney, Kirk Gerard, smacked the table before him. His copper toupee—who did he think he was fooling with that cheap thing?—flopped onto his brow. "Narrative."

I sucked in a sigh while Bob and Gerard argued to the judge about whether I would be allowed to tell my story my way—the "narrative form of testimony," Bob called it—instead of answering one tedious question after another. Bob had expected this. Prosecutors don't like narrative testimony, he said, because they can't anticipate what the witness will say next, impeding their ability to object. I think Bob liked this form of testimony for just that reason—anything to piss off Gerard and throw him off his game. I, of course, simply wanted to talk to the jury. I'd always been good at persuading people, and I knew I could do it here if I weren't constantly interrupted. Finally, after a couple of minutes, the judge ruled in our favor. Maybe Bob *was* worth his exorbitant fee.

"You can continue, Mrs. Forester," the judge said, a slight smile on his pale lips.

I nodded appreciatively, turned to the jury, and began telling my story. Quickly I got to the point.

"People keep saying I'm happy my husband is dead. The district attorney has called me a 'wealthy widow' because of the pending life insurance payment, claiming I planned all of this, instead of being the victim."

I looked right into Gerard's mean brown eyes. He had never believed my story, insisting I made it all up, that I killed Aaron for the money and staged the crime scene. But I knew the women on the jury would believe me once I explained everything. Women are very practical. I shifted my gaze back to them.

"Even my friends say I'm better off without Aaron. I'm sure they're trying to cheer me up when they remind me how he drank too much and didn't love me the way he was supposed to. *That's* clearly true, considering he tried to kill me." I paused for two full breaths to let the impact of those words sink in. "But when I lie awake late at night, I know some other truths, starting with this: I knew Aaron was *the one*, my future, from the moment we met—"

"Your Honor," the prosecutor said. "I object. Is this a murder trial or a romance novel? The defendant—"

"Overruled," the judge said. "We've gone over this already. Mrs. Forester is allowed to testify in the narrative form." He turned to me. "You may continue."

"Thank you, Your Honor." I looked at the jurors. "But even though Aaron was *the one* for me, he wasn't perfect. That's where I came in. As his wife, it was my job to help Aaron succeed in all areas of life. To prod him on. That's how we got the beach house. We bought it at my insistence. We were a successful family, with two straight-A kids, the gorgeous house in the right neighborhood. A beautiful beach house was the next step for us, even if Aaron didn't want it."

I flapped my hand. Aaron's reluctance to take our rightful place in the world still baffled me.

"He liked staycations back in Wake Forest," I said. "But we were supposed to be upwardly mobile. That's the American Dream. Getting further than your parents did. So we bought the beach house here, and everything was great for a while, until our stock portfolio took a dip. So I encouraged Aaron to apply for a promotion at work. Higher in management. In prestige. In pay. And he got it. And I was happy that my husband was succeeding, like husbands are supposed to."

I paused again, remembering our final day together, when Aaron surprised me. "Of course Aaron viewed success differently than I did. I didn't realize that then. I just thought he was a little lazy, and I had to push him to reach his full potential."

When I said the word *lazy*, I could swear I heard my mother-in-law hiss. She was sitting in the row behind the district attorney, glaring at me, her hazel eyes pinched in hatred. I had always wanted her to love me. That's how it was supposed to be. How had things turned out so wrong? Oh, yes, I had thought I could push Aaron to be a better man.

"Instead I turned him into an unhappy man," I told the jurors. "Early in our marriage, Aaron used to come home tired but invigorated by his day, eager to tell me of some new financial strategy he and his team had devised. Now I had an angry husband who came home late and spent the night drinking. He hated all the paperwork that came with being an executive. He hated the bureaucracy. And I guess he grew to hate me. Of course, I didn't realize it, not until it was too late." I shook my head. "In the end, our marriage failed because I kept trying to turn him into the man I thought he should be, instead of accepting him for who he was."

I poured myself some water from the adjacent pitcher, giving the jurors time to think about my words. Bob had advised me not to say this, not to accept any blame for what had happened. It had been self-defense, he kept reminding me. Don't give the jury an excuse to convict. But Bob was wrong. Most of the jurors were women. They would understand that helping my family flourish required me to push Aaron to grab the brass ring. They'd get how it could all go wrong.

I drank some of the tepid water—you'd think they could provide ice—then shifted toward the jurors again.

"Anyway, last summer arrived and I packed up the kids and drove to the beach house. I attended charity events with the women in town. Bought fresh fruits and vegetables at the waterfront market on Thursday mornings, when everyone shops for their organics." A couple of the jurors nodded. "I slathered on sunscreen and sat in the sand under a hat and a big umbrella, reading the latest hot novel. And I waited for the weekends for Aaron to come. I planned our days from sunrise on. The right events. The right people. The right parties. He wanted to sleep in, like the kids, but I insisted he get up early. How would it look if I went around town by myself on the weekends? So he accompanied me on my outings, and I encouraged him to be more enthusiastic about things. But I could tell he wasn't happy."

I was getting to the heart of the matter and took another good look at the jurors. They were much harder to read than I'd anticipated. At least a few seemed sympathetic—the head-tilting divorcée, the wrinkled lady with curly white hair, and the mom who was in her early forties, like me.

"In late July, I packed up the kids again and drove three hours south to my parents' retirement home near Charleston. It was Mother's birthday week. She must have sensed the strain in my marriage during that visit. She asked about the lines on my face. The faraway look in my eyes."

I glanced at my mother. She'd been sitting bravely with Daddy directly behind Bob throughout the trial. She wore the perfect dress for court, tasteful and tailored. Her silver hair was expertly coifed. But Mother was sporting new frown lines, too.

"I told Mother everything was fine. No need to worry her. I knew I could fix my marriage by having one perfect weekend with Aaron, reminding him that we were made for each other. So the day after Mother's birthday, I told her I was going back to Sunset Beach. That Aaron and I needed a romantic weekend alone."

Remembering this day was difficult. When I gazed at the courtroom now, I couldn't focus on anyone or anything. I was back at the shore in my mind, with the seagulls squawking and the air thick with moisture, a storm in the offing.

"I stopped at a little grocery store near our beach house. I bought wine and flowers and some nice salmon steaks. When I pulled into the garage in the late afternoon, I was surprised. Aaron's car was there. I'd expected to beat him by a few hours. I smoothed my blouse and skirt and went inside the house, calling for him. 'Aaron, I'm home.' But he didn't respond.

"I put the fish and wine in the refrigerator, arranged the flowers in a crystal vase, and set it on a table beside the staircase. I was about to look for Aaron on the deck when I heard music coming from upstairs. Soft and sultry. *That's* where Aaron was, I realized. He'd planned an evening of seduction. Finally he was getting with the program. This was how things were supposed to be.

"I scurried up the stairs, fluffing my hair, glad I'd worn nice lingerie. I'd only taken a couple of steps into our bedroom before something hit the back of my head hard and I blacked out. I don't think I was unconscious very long. But it was long enough for Aaron to tie me to the upholstered armchair in the corner, the rope wound around my stomach—over my clothes, where it wouldn't leave marks. When I awoke, woozy and confused, he was standing over me with a glint in his eyes as he raised our gun at my face— the one we'd gotten for home protection."

That point still galled me. I should sue that gun company. But back to Aaron.

"He told me in an ice-cold voice that he was going to kill me. 'But before I do,' he said, 'I want to make sure you know why.' Then he told me in excruciating detail how I'd enraged him every time I pushed him to achieve, as if that had been a bad thing. His voice kept rising as he went on, until he was screaming at me. He called me horrible names. For the first time, I'd wished we'd bought a home with nearby neighbors. Someone nosy who could've phoned the police."

I'd never imagined privacy would turn out to be a problem.

"Anyway, at the beginning I protested. But he shoved the gun closer, so I shut up. Its barrel seems much bigger when it's pointed at you." I sighed. "Aaron ranted about my shortcomings for a while. Then, as thunder rattled the windows, he untied me and told me to stand. Said we were going for a drive."

I half laughed, still finding it hard to believe. "He really planned to kill me. After all I'd done for him, this was how he was going to repay me. We started down the stairs, the gun pressed to my spine.

"'Move it,' he said, nudging me to walk faster.

"I twisted toward him, pleading. 'Please don't do this. We can work things out. You love me. I know you do.'

"He laughed in a cold, distant way. There was no changing his mind.

"After we reached the bottom of the staircase, I turned again. But before I could say another word, he yelled, 'Shut up, Emily. I'm tired of your bitching.' He didn't see the vase in time, not until I'd grabbed it and smacked him on the side of the head.

"Aaron fell, dropping the gun, water and flowers flying. For a moment I stood in shock, but only a moment, because Aaron opened his eyes and lunged for the gun. I snatched it off the floor, aimed, and fired.

"I'd never fired a gun before. The jolt shook my body. But nothing shook me more than watching Aaron begin to bleed as he slumped back onto the tile floor. With the gun still heavy in my hand, I ran to the phone and called the police."

Fat tears slipped onto my cheeks now, like the driving rain that had been slamming into the beach house that night, and I could see the jurors again. Wide-eyed. Mouths open. The pregnant woman held her palm over her heart. The divorcée offered me a sad smile, as did some of the men.

"It *was* self-defense," I continued. "But it was still my fault. I drove Aaron to it by not loving him enough, by not accepting him for who he was. And for that, I'm sorry."

Surely now that the jurors understood why Aaron tried to kill me, they would believe what happened and how I had no choice but to defend myself. Surely they would.

The room was silent for a few seconds but for my sniffling.

"Mrs. Forester, would you like a short break?" the judge asked.

"Yes." I nodded. "But I'm done."

"Any more questions, Mr. Gilmore?" the judge asked Bob.

"No, Your Honor."

"All right," the judge said. "We'll call it a day and resume with cross-examination at nine o'clock in the morning."

* * * *

By the time court resumed the next day, I'd gotten control of myself and was ready for the prosecutor. Good thing. Gerard came at me hard, hammering that Aaron's salary couldn't support my "expensive tastes." He claimed I pushed Aaron to seek a promotion so he'd qualify for a big life insurance policy. That I'd arranged for the kids to not be at the beach house the weekend Aaron died so no one could contradict my story. It felt like the jurors' opinion of me started to turn. Frowns creased their faces when they looked my way.

Finally Gerard finished with me, he and Bob made their closing arguments, the judge gave lengthy jury instructions, and the jurors were sent out to deliberate. Bob and I went back to his office to wait. Mother and Daddy wanted to come, but I wasn't up for company. Bob ordered in lunch, but I couldn't eat. Now that I had no more control over the verdict, my energy had evaporated.

Not three hours had passed before the court clerk called. The jury was back.

"A deliberation this short probably means a guilty verdict," Bob said. "You should prepare yourself."

No. It couldn't be.

Calmly I returned with Bob to the courtroom. Mother and Daddy smiled at me, but fear had washed the color from their faces. I was glad my children weren't there to see this. Glad my sister, Danielle, had agreed to let them stay with her back home in Wake Forest during the trial. I was even glad, for once, that Danielle drank too much, just like Aaron had. I know it sounds bad, but the kids were smart enough never to get in a car with Danielle, so they'd be safe. And they'd be preoccupied. Danielle's drinking problem would give Seth and Lucy something to worry about besides me.

Soon the jury filed in, and the judge got straight to business.

"Has the jury reached a verdict?" he asked.

"Yes, we have, Your Honor," the foreman replied.

He was lanky, a carpenter—one of the jurors I hadn't been able to read while I testified. Bob hadn't wanted him on the jury. Said he'd hate me. The way the foreman refused to meet my eyes now, I feared Bob had been right.

While a clerk handed the judge a slip of paper with the verdict on it, Bob and I stood. He touched my arm, and it felt good, reassuring, until I remembered that Aaron had touched my wrist like that during our wedding ceremony, making me feel certain our marriage would succeed. Look how well that had turned out.

The judge scanned the verdict, nodded, and the clerk returned the paper to the foreman. He rose from his seat in the jury box and began to read aloud.

"We, the jury, find the defendant, Emily Forester"—he raised his head and looked at me dead on—"not guilty."

I clapped my hand over my mouth as my mother said, "Thank God," and the courtroom audience began buzzing with a mixture of surprise, glee, and—mostly—anger. But I couldn't pay much attention to what anyone else was saying. I kept hearing the foreman's words echoing in my head.

Not guilty. Not guilty. Not guilty.

I collapsed into my chair, my eyes watering, halfway between tears and laughter. The jurors understood. They got it, even the ones I hadn't been able to read.

That's the thing about stoic people. You never really know what they're thinking.

* * * *

It's been several months since the trial, and I've become stoic, too. So I'm glad to have the chance to sit by the pool at my parents' country club tonight, watching the sun set without anyone lounging beside me, peppering me with questions about my day or telling me funny stories, trying to lighten my mood. Mother and Daddy are out ensuring everything's ready for Daddy's seventieth birthday party tomorrow. The kids are at a movie. And the other club members are the smile-and-wave kind—with me, at least. Not chatty, which I appreciate. I'm glad to have time to think.

I've spent a lot of time since the trial thinking about my life, and I realize that my marriage was doomed from the moment Aaron and I met. I pushed him to the brink. And I do take the blame for that.

But not all of it.

During his ranting and raving the day he died, Aaron revealed some things I hadn't known. He had pursued me our junior year in college because he'd thought I was *the one* for him. I checked all his boxes. Attractive, smart, determined. I'd make the perfect corporate wife, helping him raise the perfect family, he'd said. We were more alike than I'd ever imagined.

Except it turned out I had bigger dreams than he did. I wanted the beach house, trips to Europe, expensive private school for the kids, and fine clothes and jewelry for me. All Aaron wanted was a good little wife, a solid management position, and a little something on the side. I guess he thought having a mistress would make him a real man.

To add insult to injury, he didn't cheat with some random woman. He did it with my *sister*. They'd been at it for *years*. Danielle

THE POWER BEHIND THE THRONE, BY BARB GOFFMAN | 65

liked him for who he was, he said. They had *fun* together. And he'd finally decided he wanted to be with her all the time. No more harping from me. Just lots of fun with her. He didn't care how it looked. So after an appropriate mourning period, he was going to marry Danielle, without all the hassle and expense of divorce and alimony.

I hadn't mentioned this to anyone. Not my attorney or my family or my friends or the jury. I hadn't even mentioned it to Danielle, whom I tripped down the stairs at my parents' house an hour ago, right before I left for the club. She'd flailed as she began to tumble, her ever-present glass of gin crashing down the carpeted steps. A happy *thunk* sounded when Danielle's head hit the wood floor in the entryway, her neck as twisted as the staircase, with blood seeping out of her ear. I was glad I didn't need to slam her skull against the floor myself, though I'd been prepared to do it if necessary.

Mother and Daddy should be calling any time now, having found my poor dead drunk of a sister. I'm sorry to put them through this, but there really was no other way. I couldn't be the one to find the little home-wrecker, not after what happened with Aaron. Besides, Mother and Daddy are strong. They proved that during my trial. They can handle this.

As for me, I'm not sure what's next. With Seth and Lucy on track for the Ivy League, and Aaron's life insurance payout more than enough to cover their educations and keep me in the lifestyle I deserve, my future's wide open. I've already shown the world I can be a successful wife and mother—the ultimate power behind the throne. Now I'm going to take that power out for a spin, promoting the one person I've been neglecting all these years—me.

I don't know how I didn't realize it until now. *This* is how life is supposed to be.

STEWING

LIBBY HALL

They say taking down your neighbor won't bring you any higher, but the day I, Stella Dole, took down my ex-husband Scraper Dole, my level of happiness was through the roof. Our little town of Sloe in the foothills of Virginia talked for months about how Scraper had died. It was all over social media. Lordy, I still can't believe that man has a meme about him.

Before I tell you what happened, there are a couple of things you need to know. The Doles were the royalty of the poor in Sloe. When old Mayor Pritchard died, Scraper put his name down for giggles and ran against Mayor Pritchard's racist son, Dick. Of course, the old Sloe families couldn't vote for Dick because they didn't want reporters turning our town into a media circus. That's never good for business, and even worse for a town that's just starting to recover from the textile factory exodus. I don't think it surprised anyone, except Dick and Scraper, when Scraper won.

Scraper and I never had much to do with each other growing up. He started working for the county's Department of Transportation right out of high school. My parents sent me to college, and afterward I made some money selling real estate in Richmond. When my folks passed, I came back to Sloe and used family money to develop two new retirement communities along the river.

After Scraper settled into the mayor's office, I called on him for a special building permit, bringing him a shepherd's pie to seal the deal. I'm known for my shepherd's pies—I bring them to every potluck and funeral. I use steak, not just stew meat, or venison when I can get it. Scraper loved my pies. Long story short, between my flattering him and giving him the pie, the permit was a done deal.

Scraper was annoying, and tons smarter than he acted, and the man had a sex appeal that I still don't understand. I usually like my men young, easy to manage, and temporary. Scraper was none of those things. Somehow three dinners, two more pies, one permit, and lots of dirty sex later, we got married.

Oh, we fought more than two cats in a bag. The man infuriated me from the start. Several times he brought home roadkill from work, always claimed it was "fresh" and I could use it in one of my pies. I don't care how "fresh" it was—I never cooked roadkill.

It took three years, more fighting and an affair before we divorced. The day I signed the papers, I sent one of my employees over to his office with another shepherd's pie to say goodbye. The marriage might have ended, but we couldn't stop poking at each other like kids at a hornet nest.

I look pretty good for forty. My blond hair, long legs, good tan, and flat stomach mean I never have to work too hard to get a date. I like my freedom, but in a small town, there are reminders of your mistakes everywhere. And right now, the biggest reminder of all was leaning against my new Cadillac when I closed up my office.

"Get off my car, Scraper. I can smell you from here."

Scraper stayed where he was and tilted his head up. "I don't see how. Your perfume would knock a man over at fifty feet."

"You can't smell anything." It was true, and it was why he was also the DOT's go-to man for scraping dead animals off the roads. I tried to shove him away from the car. "I don't have time for this."

He stayed put, smiling. "I was just thinking about you, lovey. You know that big stand of trees on the slope by the stream? I'm going to cut 'em down. I can't really see the river all that well."

After our divorce, Scraper started renting the house on the slope above mine, to get back at me, I'm sure, but since we didn't see much of each other, it was easy to ignore him.

"You know damn well my Daddy planted those trees," I said. "I'll have you fined for destroying a… a… environmental habitat or something!"

Scraper laughed. "That's rich, coming from the chief developer of—what is it? Sleepy Hollow Hills or some suburban crap like that? Nothing you file will hold any water here. Too many folks hate you for bringing in all those outsiders." He paused. "You hear Dallas Chirp is back in town? I hired him, you know—figured nobody else would, after everything that happened between you two. Every good deed deserves another, don't you think?"

Dallas Chirp had slunk out of Sloe ten years ago after brawling with my lover, Tom Slaughter. Tom and I were "visiting" the motel where Dallas worked and he spotted us. They got into a fight and it spilled into the street. Tom wound up with a broken arm and thirty-five stitches in his head. Dallas got fired, and I had to explain in court why I was at the Stars & Stripes Motel with someone other than Scraper. For months afterward, my life was nothing but gossip and "Bless her heart" comments. I laid low, moved out, and started fixing up the old family home outside of town until things blew over.

"That boy deserves better than he got," I said. "Maybe I'll see what I can do for him too. Now get off my car, or I'll run you over."

Scraper slowly stretched and stepped away. I gunned the engine as I left, hoping some of the smaller rocks would hit him.

The next evening, I tracked Dallas Chirp down in the Shook Nook, a local crab shack on the river. It wasn't hard—his truck's license plate read "CHIRP 1." After convincing him there weren't any hard feelings and that I just wanted to help him get a fresh start, he agreed to come do some work for me until he could find something permanent. What I didn't count on was how much he'd grown up in ten years. The gangly, pimply-faced kid from the motel had turned into a man with scruffy hair, arms like Popeye, and a chest you just wanted to run your hands down for fun. And he met all my criteria—handsome, dumb, and temporary. Many drinks later, I found myself with a new yardman and an energetic lover.

I don't know whether Scraper saw Dallas' truck in my driveway that night or not, but I know he saw Dallas come over the next day to start work. I could see the sun glinting off Scraper's binoculars. Pervert.

When Dallas had gone, I did what I always do in the summer afternoons. I carried a towel and a book across the lawn to my tanning chair. Sure enough, those binoculars were busy again. Minutes later, a golf ball landed in my yard. I heard the thump and looked up, but it had settled in the grass, so I went back to my book. Scraper put another ball on the ground and swung again, softer this time. I looked up as the ball hooked to the right. Scraper waved.

You have to ignore childish behavior to take the fun out of it, so I went back to my book.

Thwack!

When the next golf ball landed three feet away, I jumped out of my chair.

"Dammit, Scraper! My yard is not your private golf course!"

"Sorry, sweetheart," he called back. "Didn't see you. I was just practicing for my meeting with the county planners next week."

"What meeting?" County planners were the key to the next step of my development.

"To decide whether or not the county can afford all the schools and roads those new houses of yours are going to require. You know, all that zoning crap you developers hate so much?"

"Scraper Dole, I swear to God if you try and stop me from—"

"Relax, hon. I ain't telling them nothing yet. But maybe your new lawn boy can help you. I hear he's the owner of some prime real estate. It sure would be awfully convenient to have him sell you that property."

"I don't know what you're talking about."

Of course, I did. I needed the acreage from Dallas' grandparents' place for the development. Believe me, I wasn't hiring him or sleeping with him just to be nice. That acreage was the only thing standing in the way of the zoning restrictions already in place. Dallas' grandparents were old school and wouldn't sell at any price. My only other move was to get the zoning changed. I'd spent the last two years promising the zoning board the moon, but they kept stalling, and Scraper was at the bottom of it. If the zoning board didn't vote my way, I wouldn't be able to create the family neighborhood that Sloe needed to feed into the new hospital system being built in Verna, five miles down the highway. I needed Dallas to sell me that land he'd inherited.

"You better watch your step, Stella. That boy might hoe a row better than you."

I grabbed my things, gave Scraper the finger and stomped back to the house.

The warning reminded me of something Dallas had told me last week when he'd been edging Scraper's lawn. Seems Scraper had built a catapult from scraps of wood and an old bike tire. According to Dallas, the catapult had a tarp next to it, covering a pile of his three dogs' poop. Scraper had been sitting in his lawn chair, a pair of binoculars hung from his neck, Dallas said. He went on to detail their exchange.

"What is that?" Dallas had asked, pointing at the tarp.

"What's it look like?"

"A big pile of poop. Jesus, Scraper, how can you just sit there?"

Scraper shrugged. "Lost my sense of smell a long time ago in a fight. That's why I pick up the road kill. Watch this."

He shoveled a pile of filth onto the arm of the catapult, strapped the arm back, and flicked away an elastic band. The arm of the catapult snapped forward, pitching its load into the air. Scraper handed Dallas the binoculars to view the results. Brown clumps surrounded my tanning chair.

"I think you hit a foot or two to the left," Dallas said. "Don't you think she'll call the police or something?"

"She won't. The sheriff owes me too many favors." Scraper glanced sideways at Dallas and smiled, but Dallas said it never quite reached his eyes. "Besides, she slept with half of the deputies and dumped them when she was done. None of them will write a report about something as stupid as dog poop in her yard."

"You looking out for me, Scraper, or was that a warning?" Dallas asked.

"Just a little friendly advice. You humiliated her a long time ago. Don't think she's forgotten it."

When Dallas told me that, I shrugged it off but, like I said, Scraper isn't as dumb as he pretends to be.

I didn't say anything to Dallas and tried to pretend it didn't bother me. If Dallas was telling me about Scraper's plan, what was he telling Scraper about me? But the next incident was the last straw.

A couple of days later, while I was at my yoga class, Dallas went to work and found Scraper sitting next to the tarp again, catapult ready. On the tarp was a pile of dead dogs, two squirrels, and an opossum.

"You got to be kidding," Dallas muttered.

Scraper turned in his chair and waved him over to his cooler. "Grab a beer. I got something I want to show you. I ain't had time to try it out yet."

Scraper handed him the binoculars and his beer. "Watch this." He picked up one of the dogs. It was frozen stiff.

"You froze them?" Dallas asked, incredulous.

Scraper nodded. "They'll fling better."

Scraper loaded the dog carcass onto the catapult, pulled the lever back and launched it into my yard. It landed a short distance from my chair.

"You sure she's not home?" Dallas asked.

"Yep." He loaded one of the squirrels onto the catapult and launched. "Damn, too short." He loaded an opossum and launched again. It landed a few feet from the dog. "That'll work. I just want her to be able to smell 'em when she gets outside. She used to hate that smell when I got off work. She didn't like that part of my job," Scraper mused out loud, "but she sure liked a challenge. She never could make me do what she wanted."

"So now you're throwing dead dogs in her yard?"

"Don't lecture me on my ex-wife, son. Just because you're the flavor of the month don't mean you understand."

"If you think I'm going to let you throw more crap in her yard when I have to clean it up, you're wrong," Dallas said.

"What are you going do about it? You gonna throw me through a glass window like you did Tom Slaughter?"

Dallas said he tried to rein in his rage, but he smashed Scraper's nose anyway. While Scraper howled and tried to stop the flow of blood, Dallas got in his truck and left. He came to my house that night, and after we made love, he told me what had happened. I didn't say much, but inside I was seething. Dallas must have known the night was ruined, because he got dressed and practically ran out the door.

The next morning, I found him staining chairs in his garage.

"I need you to do some work for me today," I said.

He ignored me, moving wood around. Well, I'm not that easy to get rid of, and the bottom line is, he was still my employee.

"Dallas, I've got a yard full of dead animals. I need them cleaned up."

Dallas looked up. "I'm not cleaning them up. Scraper's deliberately doing this stuff because he knows he can get to us both."

"Well, what am I supposed to do?"

He sighed. "I'll come by after lunch and dig a hole for you. But that's it. I'm not getting stuck in the middle of whatever it is you two are doing anymore."

"But *I'm* not doing anything! It's all him!"

He straightened up and said, "You two have been fighting World War Three for years. And I see now I'm just the latest weapon."

"That's not true," I lied.

"I know why you hired me. I'm not selling my grandparents' farm. Not to you. Not to nobody." He crossed his arms and stared at me, hard, with his lips pressed hard together. Any other day I would have melted. He looked incredibly sexy like that.

Instead, I saw red. That little troublemaker was *not* going to ruin my plans, and I was going to kill whoever told him about the zoning problems I was having. "After I gave you a job when nobody else would, and let you in my house—"

"Me and apparently every man you hire," he said. "I might work construction and landscaping, Stella, but I'm not stupid. Now, I said I'd dig you a hole, and I will, but that's all. Burying road kill is not part of the deal. Scraper knew you'd try to make me clean it up. That's my punishment for being with you." He made a show of clamping a new piece of wood and picking up the sander. "I'm not touching them."

He switched on the sander, drowning out anything I was going to say.

That night I sat and fumed. In my heart, I knew Dallas wasn't to blame. Scraper and I had played him like a fiddle. Once again that man had pissed in my pot and ruined the only good thing I had going. I'd used all my equity and borrowing power to buy that land to develop it. If Dallas wouldn't sell his granddad's land and Scraper controlled the zoning, I was going to end up sitting on a 300-acre piece of dirt. With no houses on it, I'd be lucky if I could sell it at all, much less break even.

I thought for a long time about my options. The idea of making nice with Scraper turned my stomach, but in the end, I knew the only way I was going to get what I needed was to make peace. Even if Dallas sold me his property, the zoning would still be a problem if Scraper wanted it to be. Scraper had to think I was giving up the fight, and nothing would make him happier than thinking he'd finally beaten me. And I knew the perfect thing to take him as a peace offering.

Dallas did what he said he'd do and dug a hole for the carcasses. I went out that evening and threw the stinking animals into it, except for one opossum. I took the opossum to my kitchen and took a set of piecrusts out to thaw, until I remembered that everybody knows shepherd's pies are my go-to food gift. I put the crusts back and made a stew instead, heavy on the beans and spices the way Scraper liked. I added chunks of the 'possum at the tail end of the cooking process, for the gamey flavor he liked. Who's to say if they cooked all the way through or not?

The next evening, I put the stew in a disposable container, wiped it down, put it in a gift bag, and drove up to Scraper's. The catapult was still in the yard, aimed at my house.

"Well, well, well," Scraper said when he answered my knock. "If it ain't Mrs. Robinson. To what do I owe this honor?" I ignored the sarcasm and braced myself for what I was about to say, hoping I wouldn't actually choke on the words.

"Scraper, I think we need to call a truce," I said quietly. He raised his eyebrows but didn't say anything. I shifted my feet and looked at the floor like I practiced. "Look, I handled things badly when we were married, and God knows I'm still doing it. You bring out the absolute worst in me, but this isn't how I want to live."

"You call that an apology?" he asked. He started to close the door, but I stuck my arm out.

I felt my face get red, but I took a deep breath and pushed against the door with my free hand, so he couldn't close it. "Scraper, wait!"

I made my voice hitch just a little, like I was about to cry. "Tom Slaughter was a mistake, and I know I've only made it worse by parading my… friends in front of you. You don't deserve that." I looked down, hoping I looked sorry. When I looked back up, I had managed to wet my eyes just a little. Scraper stared at me silently for a full ten seconds, then reached out and took the stew. "What is it?" he asked.

"It's stew. I was going to make a pie like old times, but I didn't have any crusts."

I swear the man smiled just a bit. "Well, it ain't pie, but you know I like your cooking." He stretched out a hand. "Truce?"

I grabbed it and shook it. "Truce."

They found Scraper a few days later, sprawled in his bed, vomit all over everything. There was an empty, disposable container in the trash and a dirty bowl in the sink. I didn't hear about it until Frances Townsend, fresh from Sheriff Tate's office where she worked part-time, came into my office and said, "Oh Stella, I am so sorry to hear about Scraper."

"What do you mean?" I asked innocently, coming around my desk.

She laid a soft, plump hand on my shoulder. "Oh, honey, they haven't told you yet?" I shook my head. "Scraper passed away a couple of days ago."

I sat back in my chair and stared. I opened my mouth and closed it a couple of times to make sure she knew I was shocked.

"What do you mean?"

Frances nodded sympathetically, but I knew she was relishing every detail and would spread it around town faster than green grass through a goose. "It's such a shock, I know. Apparently, it was food poisoning." She gave me the details of what they found, while I continued to look shocked.

"That poor man," I said. "Bless his heart, when we were married he was always trying to get me to cook up some poor animal he'd scraped off the road, saying it was still good. Of course, I flat out refused. Everybody knows it isn't safe." I wiped an imaginary tear from my eyes.

"Oh, Stella, I'm so sorry. Can I get you anything?"

I shook my head. "I just need to be alone for a while, I think, Frances."

"Of course, sugar. You just call me when you're ready to hear the details for the service."

Frances gave me an awkward hug and left the office. I looked down at the aerial plans for the new community and smiled.

SHADOW MAN

BRAD HARPER

"Tell me a story, Grandma. I'd like one with a witch in it this time."

Seven-year-old Tommy was bargaining with his Grandmother Buford, trying his best to hold off his bedtime. There was a monster under his bed, he was sure of it. Sometimes in the middle of the night he heard a noise like little claws scrabbling on the smooth floor. Once when half-awake, he thought he saw a claw peek out as he leaned over, but whatever it was jerked back into darkness when he gasped.

So he decided the later he went to bed, the faster he would go to sleep and the less time for the monster to get him. It was well known that monsters that live in closets and beneath beds only feed on those awake. He also hoped that a good story from his grandmother would help him escape into dreamland as soon as his head hit the pillow.

"What story would that be?" asked Grandma in her creaking rocking chair, her faded black shawl around her shoulders, her wrinkled face pink and shiny by the fire. "How about Hansel and Gretel? That has a witch in it."

Tommy pouted, his lower lip protruding into what Grandma Buford called his Liverwurst Lip. "That's a children's story, Grandma! I'm too old for that. Tell me a *real* story."

Grandma spread her hands in mock surrender. "All right, Big Boy, a real story it is, but be careful what you wish for! Now go dress for bed, and I'll tell you a true story about a robber who stole too much. It's a family legend, and part of it happened in this very house, so I reckon it's time you heard it."

"In this house?" He asked, his mouth open, his lip returned to its normal size. "Is there a witch in it?"

"Oh yes, dear. A witch, a robber, magical potions, demons, and your great-great-grandfather. Now get ready, young man, before I change my mind!"

Tommy hurried up the stairs to his room, careful not to spill any wax from his candle on the carpeted staircase, and soon he was back, dressed in his red flannel nightshirt and thick woolen socks, his blue eyes shining with excitement. "I'm ready, Grandma! Now start, please?"

Grandma smiled at his sudden outburst of good behavior as she poured herself a glass of elderberry wine from the dusty crystal decanter. For her rheumatism, of course. She pondered how to begin as she studied the firelight darting through the dark liquid in her glass. "Long ago in the bayou there lived a highwayman..."

"A robber, Grandma, you said a robber!" Tommy said, his lower lip peeking out once more.

"Yes, Tommy, a highwayman is a kind of robber, one who steals from travelers using his sword and pistol to make them give up their money or anything else of value when he stops them on the road. Now, be quiet and listen, or I'll stop right here."

Little Tommy tucked his feet under him and held his knees tight, his eyes wide open as his grandmother told her tale, the low fire casting her face in alternating shadow and light. Soon her soft voice carried him to a time before even this ancient storyteller was born.

"This highwayman was a very greedy man who took from everyone he caught. Others would not rob widows or poor people, but this man would take the last penny from a starving child. He was hated for he was cruel, but feared even more, because he was very cruel."

"How was he cruel, Grandma?"

"He once robbed a poor box in a church, which was bad enough, but when the priest caught him, he cut off the priest's nose before he ran away laughing. No one dared follow him into the night, and he got away scot-free."

"Nobody tried to catch him, ever?"

"Now don't rush me Tommy, I'm getting to that, but no one did for a very long time even though there was a large bounty on his head."

"What's a bounty?"

"A reward for his capture. Old Man Buford, your great-great-grandfather, put it there after he was robbed at sword point. The robber was so feared no one even spoke his name, so he was called the Shadow Man, for he was never seen in daylight."

"Shadow Man," Tommy whispered and shivered by the fire, hugging his knees tighter.

"That's right, Shadow Man. He was always dressed in black, rode on a swift, black horse, and no one ever saw him coming. He was so feared that when he yelled out 'Stand and deliver!' his victims never dared fight back, not even full-grown men, and they all gave him their money straightaway."

When Grandma said "stand and deliver," Tommy imagined the Shadow Man standing before him on a dark road, the blade of his sword glimmering beneath a pale moon, inches from Tommy's own face. He wiggled in delight, and his heart beat faster. "So who did fight back? The sheriff? Did he form a posse?"

"Even the sheriff was too afraid, Tommy, and no one would join his posse if he'd tried. Now be patient!

"In those days there were witches in the bayous here about. Some were bad, but most just wanted to be left alone. The witch in our story was named Spinner because of the magical dreams her potions would spin. They said she spun those spells just like a spider spins its web. Some dreams she made would tell the future, some would bring good luck, and some eased the passage into the next world where all dreams end.

"One moonless night, Shadow Man came to Spinner's shack while she was out gathering herbs and took all the money she had been given for her bottles filled with dreams. It was a lot of gold, I can tell you, and when she found it gone, the sound of her anger frightened the swamp into silence for miles around. I'm told even the 'gators hid in their dens at the sound of her curses."

"Wow! Nothing scares a 'gator, 'cept a *bigger* 'gator! Then what happened?"

Grandma Buford laughed, enjoying how her grandson was hanging on every word. She couldn't stay angry at him, no matter how much he interrupted.

"I was getting to that, now hush!" she said, feigning sternness. "Spinner must have gone on caterwauling for half the night before she finally hushed up. They say the silence was scarier than the sound of her screams. For three days and nights she read her books of dark magic and summoned demons to guide her as she plotted her revenge on Shadow Man, for she knew that only he would dare to steal her gold."

Tommy was now at her feet, his back to the fire as he stared up at Grandma Buford, imagining a witch far off in the bayous talking to horned demons with yellow teeth and sulfurous breath. The dancing shadows in the parlor seemed to grow horns of their own and he started when a log in the fire suddenly popped. He thought of a fire much hotter far below where demons lived and wasn't sure he wanted Grandma to go on. But he swallowed and stayed silent, afraid to break her spell.

"When those three days had passed," Grandma said, leaning forward and speaking in a low voice, "the smoke was still thick over her shack as Spinner brewed a black liquid in her large and glowing kettle. When she was finished, she went to Old Man Buford, and after a long private conversation, she returned to her little house in the swamp, driving the Buford family carriage with its two matched mares. Meanwhile, Old Man Buford paid for some of his servants to go to the local taverns and tell stories about a love affair between his son and a mysterious young lady who lived near the bayou.

"Shadow Man laughed as he spent Spinner's gold on gambling and other things that robbers like, but which you are too young to understand, and though he had stolen a lot of gold, he soon found he was poor again. Then Shadow Man heard rumors that Old Man Buford's son, your great-grandfather, had a lady friend he visited once a month in a cottage at the edge of the swamp. The stories said he would ride to her on the first night the moon was full, which was in fact that very night. Shadow Man smiled as he sharpened his sword, cleaned his pistol, and blackened his face to make himself ready. Then he muffled the hooves of his horse so that he could move without making a noise and rode out to wait in the dark, along the trail to the secret cottage the Buford servants had talked about.

"Around midnight the Buford carriage came down the trail just as he'd expected, and when the highwayman blocked the road, it stopped, the coachman throwing up his hands when Shadow Man shouted out, "Stand and deliver!" as he always did. He threw open the door of the carriage, expecting to see a frightened rich man inside, but found Spinner instead, smiling at him. 'Give me back my gold and live,' she said, 'or you will never see the sun again.'

"Shadow Man laughed at her, 'I don't see the sun now, you old hag, and soon neither will you!'

"With that he ran his sword through her, but instead of blood, he found straw, for the witch had turned into a scarecrow right before his eyes! He looked up to the coachman and saw her in the driver's seat just before she dashed a black potion into his eyes."

"What happened then, Grandma? Did Shadow Man die?"

"No one knows, Tommy. But the next day Spinner returned here to the Buford Mansion driving the carriage and carrying a small birdcage covered in black cloth. When she met with Old Man Buford he refused to give her the reward for the highwayman, saying he didn't want anything to do with black magic. In a fury, Spinner cursed him and his descendants with sleepless nights. Then she opened the cage, threw it in the wine cellar and stomped out of the mansion."

"Then what happened?"

"Well, Old Man Buford had change of heart the next morning about cheating a witch, so later he sent men with the reward to her shack. But her house was gone."

"Where was it?"

"Don't know. It was as though the swamp ate her, the house and maybe even Shadow Man up."

"That's a great story, Grandma! It's much better than Hansel and Gretel. But what's a descendent?"

Grandma Buford sighed. "It means those who come after. Since Old Man Buford was your great-great-grandfather, that means you."

"I love the story. Will you tell it to me again tomorrow night?"

"Perhaps, but now it's time for bed, Tommy. Don't worry Big Boy, I'll tuck you in."

Tommy's eyes grew wide. "I'm scared to go to bed."

"Why is that, dear?"

Tommy looked down at the floor, doing his best to act like a big boy. "Because I have a monster under my bed." He swallowed. "He scares me!"

Grandma smiled, showing the half-dozen or so teeth she had left. "I think I have an answer for that. For every poison, there's an antidote. For every curse, there's a cure. Trust me."

The procession to bed went as smoothly as it ever did, and finally, after a drink of water, a trip to the bathroom, and a goodnight kiss, Tommy was in bed. Before blowing out his candle, Grandma Buford vanished and then quickly returned with a birdcage covered in faded black cloth. She placed it on the floor beside his bed and opened the cage door. "This will keep you safe."

"What is it?" he asked.

"It catches monsters." She kissed him one more time and left.

Tommy began to doze off, when suddenly he sat bolt upright. Was it his imagination, or did he hear scuffling beneath the bed?

He took a deep breath and looked over the edge and down into the darkness. A small, dark claw extended from beneath the bed, and Tommy's heart hammered as two glowing eyes blinked back at him. Then the eyes turned towards the cage and narrowed. There was a sharp squeak, and the claw and eyes withdrew with a quick scrabbling sound that quickly faded away, never to return.

Perhaps Shadow Man recognized the cage designed by a witch's spell to imprison him and was frightened away. Or perhaps another kind of spell, cast by a loving grandmother's story, banished the monster in Tommy's mind.

I'll leave it to you to decide, but from then on Tommy slept peacefully through the night, undisturbed.

COUNTRY SONG GONE WRONG

SHERRY HARRIS
Guest Author

For the first time since Sarah Winston had started her garage sale business she was stuck doing a sale she didn't want to do. "Are you sure you want to sell all of this?" Sarah asked her client. She stood in an enormous family room.

"You bet your cotton pickin' heart I do," June Baby Pickens replied.

Sarah looked over at her friend, Carol Carson. They'd known June since before she was June Baby Pickens, the famous country western song writer married to Roydon Pickens, the famous country singer. The couple lived in a mansion in Virginia horse country with rolling hills and the Shenandoah Valley as a backdrop.

"Even Roydon's platinum record award?" Carol asked.

"Yes. You can't run off with the nanny and disappear without expecting to be humiliated in return. Mark it one dollar."

Roydon had taken off almost a week ago. June had found a note saying he'd fallen for the nanny. That he was sorry—as if that would fix things.

"Where are the kids?" Sarah asked.

"I sent them to my mom's house in Monterey." Monterey is where they'd all met nineteen years ago. June had sung in a little bayside bar. Her voice had been good enough for that, but not good enough for Nashville. Roydon, who was twenty years older, had been there on vacation. They'd fallen for each other and soon June was living in Virginia writing hits for Roydon like "Take My Heart, Leave the Dog" and "I Didn't Know Stupid Until I Married You."

June swiped at her eyes. Sarah worried about the dark circles. She'd gotten used to seeing June on TV with big hair, dripping in makeup and diamonds, Roydon at her side. June had asked Sarah to run a garage sale for her to get rid of what Roydon had left behind. Which, looking around the house, was almost everything. Very odd. Sarah had brought Carol along to help with the sale and keep June company.

"He made me a cliché. I hate him." June gave up swiping at the tears. "I don't hate him. I still love him. More than a damn viper loves its poison." She paused, screwed her face into a thoughtful look. "Maybe I should write that song. Listen to me. Everything sounds like a song to me."

They stood in Roydon's study. "You're going to get rid of that guitar? The one signed by Johnny Cash. At a *garage* sale. It's probably worth a lot of money," Sarah said. Even though the area was rural, people would flock to this garage sale once word got out.

"I don't need the money. I need revenge. Hmm, maybe that should be my next song. What do you think?"

Carol and Sarah looked at each other. "It sounds good?" Carol's voice went up on the word "good."

"You're sure Roydon doesn't want any of this stuff?" Sarah asked again. Roydon had walked away not only from his family, but everything else in his life. It didn't make sense, even after June had shown Sarah the emails from Roydon saying he didn't want any of it.

That night they sat around the kitchen island. One that was so big it really could be an island.

"I'm writing a new song," June said.

Sarah thought that was a good sign. Anything to get June's mind off the nanny. "Tell us about it."

"It's called 'You Made My Halo Crack.' It's a song of love, betrayal, and revenge."

Sarah and Carol exchanged glances. "It must be therapeutic," Carol said.

"Damn right. It's perfect for Carrie Underwood. She loves a good revenge song."

"I just don't get it," Sarah said. "Roydon's always been so crazy for you."

"Yeah, well now he's just crazy. Maybe that would be a good song 'Now He's Just Crazy.'"

"Are you sure?" Carol asked.

"After he left I found a burner phone in his study. Full of torrid text messages."

This was hard to ask, but something nagged at Sarah. A burner phone carelessly left out. Roydon didn't want any of his things. It just didn't add up. "Were there any, uh, personal photos?"

"No, but the messages said it all."

"When's the last time you talked to him?" Sarah asked.

"I haven't. We are corresponding through email."

Sarah thought that anyone could send an email. "And when's the last time he talked to the kids?"

Tears spilled out of June's eyes. The first full on tears Sarah had seen since they'd arrived. Before this she'd been pissed. Her lip quivered. "He hasn't." The tears overflowed, followed by sobs, and a gut-wrenching moan.

Carol glared at Sarah across the island. "I'm sorry, June." Sarah reached over and patted her hand.

A "yoo-hoo" from the back door saved them. A redhead with big hair and too much makeup walked in and set a bottle of bourbon in the middle of the isle. "Looks like y'all need some of this."

"Hey, Ella Mae," June said, "Let me grab some glasses."

"I'll get them for you," Ella Mae sashayed over to a cabinet and grabbed four on-the-rocks glasses.

They'd met Ella Mae yesterday when they arrived. She'd been "keeping company," as she said, with June like someone had died. Ella Mae was June's closest neighbor. You could see her house on a crest of a hill across the way.

Ella Mae splashed bourbon into four glasses giving June a heavy pour. Bourbon wasn't Sarah's favorite, but she put on her game face. She'd already made June cry once and didn't want to do it again. After they clinked glasses, Sarah knocked back a tiny bit of the bourbon.

"Now, June honey, why on earth are you crying?" Ella Mae asked. "Roydon ain't worth crying over."

"You're right, Ella Mae. You always have been." She took another large swallow, intercepting the raised-eyebrows look Carol and Sarah exchanged. "Ella Mae's my best friend ever since I moved here."

Sarah had heard all about Ella Mae over the years. She'd greeted June, delighted to have a new neighbor close to her age. They had their babies at about the same time, took care of each other, went horseback riding together, and shared their secrets. June was lucky to have her.

"Ella Mae told me early on that Roydon had a wandering eye. She wasn't the only one around here that warned me Roydon fell hard and left easy. Hey, that would make a good song."

"But you are the only one he married," Carol said.

"And you stayed married a long time," Sarah added.

June's eyes watered again and Ella Mae gave Sarah a 'what the hell' look.

"Hey, June do you remember the time…" Sarah started off with a tale about a night that Carol, June, and she had decided a late-night dip in Monterey Bay was a good idea—until the sheriff's deputy arrived.

"Remember how June buckled her knees. That young deputy almost had a heart attack trying to catch June before she hit the sand?" Carol said.

"Well, he let us go, didn't he?" June said.

"After he got your number," Sarah added.

They spent the rest of the evening drinking bourbon and laughing over crazy things they did when they were young. It was like a tonic.

Sarah walked Ella Mae to the door as Carol and June said their goodnights and went upstairs. "Keep June out of the nanny's room if you can," Ella Mae said.

"Why?"

Ella Mae shuddered. "She was obsessed with Roydon. There's pictures of him plastered everywhere. I went up there to search for clues of their whereabouts right after they first took off." Ella Mae shook her head. "It's bad. I plan to clear it out for June but haven't been able to sneak back over. Maybe you can do it and save June from seeing it."

* * * *

Sarah went up to Roydon's study. She'd been in here on a past visit, and it hadn't changed much. The walls were lined with photos of June and the kids. Yes, there were also some mementos of his singing career, but the room was more homage to his family than anything else. Old maps lined one wall. Why would a man who had a room like this run off with the nanny?

Sarah knew celebrity marriages weren't easy and lord knows Roydon had his faults. He had a big ego, but when it came to June and the kids, he had always put them first. Roydon hadn't had a big hit in five years, hadn't been nominated for an award for six. Did the nanny stroke his ego and fill something empty in him? Maybe Sarah could slow this whole garage sale thing down until she had more answers or until Roydon came to his senses.

Sarah had one more stop before she headed to bed. She grabbed keys off the hook by the back door and climbed the steps to the apartment above the garage where the nanny had lived. Seconds later she stood in the middle of the nanny's room. *Holy crap.* Sarah turned in a slow circle of the spacious studio apartment. Almost every inch of wall space was posters or framed pictures of Roydon. Some had been printed out and some had June cut out. Others were pictures of the nanny laughing with the kids and Roydon. Pictures that June must have taken.

The nanny was cute but not a stunner. She wasn't the young ingénue that Sarah had expected. She was just on the far side of plump, but it suited her. She did have dark eyes, gorgeous thick hair, and lush lips. Dimples lent her face a happy look. But the way she'd betrayed June and the kids meant her heart must be darker than mountain shadows.

Sarah started going through the room methodically—a skill she'd learned doing garage sales. Halfway through, she realized she was too tired to finish. So groggy that she wouldn't know if she'd found anything important. She decided to call it a night.

As Sarah left the nanny's room, she wondered if June had known just how obsessed the nanny had been with Roydon. It was scary, and it left Sarah wondering if all was as it seemed, or if something else was at play here. The idea that Roydon would run off with the obsessed nanny didn't sit well. Sarah crept back to her own room, plagued by questions. Questions she needed to ask June but was hesitant to. June might be full of bravado, but Sarah knew she was fragile. Who wouldn't be under the circumstances?

* * * *

The next morning Carol was sitting alone at the big island when Sarah walked into the kitchen, grabbed a cup, and poured coffee. A plate of croissants sat in the middle of the island. She snagged one and put it on a small plate. Next to Carol was an empty coffee mug with June's favorite shade of lipstick on the rim. A croissant sat on a plate beside it, crumbled to pieces, but not eaten.

"Where's June?" Sarah asked.

"She and Ella Mae took the horses out for a morning ride," Carol said.

"I'm glad she's keeping up some routine. Her days must be pretty empty without Roydon and the kids here."

Carol nodded. She had a husband and kids of her own.

"Carol, I think something is off here."

"No kidding. Roydon's a dick."

"That's not what I mean. I'm starting to wonder if he left on his own."

"What are you talking about?"

"Don't you think it's strange that no one has heard from him except through emails?"

Carol shrugged. "Not especially."

"He loved June. And even if he left *her*, I can't imagine him cutting the kids out of his life."

Carol frowned. "Roydon was always crazy about them." Carol chewed her croissant while she puzzled over what Sarah had just said. "What's your point?"

"I'm not sure, but what if he didn't leave voluntarily. What if the nanny kidnapped him?" Sarah sipped her coffee watching Carol over the rim of the cup.

Her face turned a pasty color. "What even gave you that idea?"

"Come with me. You need to see the nanny's room. It's disturbing."

Sarah flung the door open and let Carol go in first. Carol stood in the middle of the room and turned a slow circle just like Sarah had the night before. She watched Carol take in the pictures, watched emotions flicker across her face. "Are you going to tell June about this?" Carol asked.

"Not until I know more."

"Yeah, if you were wrong it would only make things worse."

"Way to make me feel better." But Sarah knew Carol was right.

"How do you plan to figure this out?"

"While I'm pricing things for the garage sale, I'm going to be searching for clues."

"What are you looking for?" Carol asked.

"Anything that will tell us where they could be."

Carol glanced at her watch. "We've got about fifteen minutes before June comes back. I don't want her to find us up here."

"I hear you. I'd love to take all these pictures down so June doesn't have to deal with it."

"Why don't we?" Carol asked.

"Because it might be part of a crime scene. We have to figure out what happened first."

They searched for ten minutes before Sarah held up a passport. "Look! It's the nanny's. Looks like they didn't flee the country at least."

"Do you know where the nanny is originally from?" Carol asked.

"I found some paperwork last night that said Minnesota. June used an agency to hire her."

"And you always hear how nice people from Minnesota are. All that water and fresh air." Carol paused. "Are you sure you don't just wish that Roydon hadn't run off with the nanny. That you aren't just trying to make things right for June? Remember she found that phone with the text messages."

"Messages but no pictures," Sarah said. "It would be easy to pick up a couple phones and fake messages back and forth between them. Then plant one of them."

"But why do that?"

"To make June believe the narrative. That Roydon's a cheat who fell in love with the nanny."

"That's one diabolical nanny." Carol didn't sound convinced. "We'd better put the rest of our search on hold. Let's go back to the house and start pricing things. Maybe something will come to us."

* * * *

Sarah had been working in Roydon's study all morning. She was certain that if there was a clue around, it had to be in here. She'd already searched his desk. Thank heavens for the wooden floors in hall. June's heels clicked down them and alerted Sarah before June came in.

"June, this picture is an original oil painting. It's worth around twenty thousand dollars." Sarah had looked it up online when she recognized the artist's name.

"Put fifteen on it," June said. "It's one of his favorites."

"*Fifteen dollars?*" Maybe Sarah should buy it all and give it back when June and Roydon came to their senses. Surely, one of them would.

No use arguing now. Sarah drifted over to the old maps. "These look really old." They were hand drawn on old parchment paper. Yellowed with age.

"Oh, they are. They're from his great, great, great granddaddy's homestead."

Sarah studied the maps. One of them had streams and forests and little buildings scattered across it. Things were marked—Ford Creek, Pickens Cabin, Washington's Woods. "I'm just going to try to figure out a price on this," she told June.

As soon as June left, Sarah brought up a maps program on her phone. From what she could tell, if the Pickens cabin was still there, it was only about ten miles from here.

* * * *

Twenty minutes later Carol and Sarah bumped down a dirt road with more ridges than an antique washboard. Trees were thick and flamed with fall colors.

"Good lord. It feels like my head is going to rattle off," Carol said.

Sarah kept a tight grip on the wheel of Roydon's red pickup. "Look. There's the cabin." The porch slumped to the right and the roof sagged to the left. Sarah pulled the truck off the road. "We'd better walk from here."

"I don't see any cars or signs of life."

"I might be wrong, but what better place to stash someone?" It was quiet out here. The creepy kind of quiet or maybe Sarah was just to used to living in a metropolitan area where there was always some level of noise. "Maybe we should take something with us." Sarah looked in the bed of the pickup truck. There was fishing gear, a collapsible shovel, and a heavy-duty flashlight. Sarah tossed the flashlight to Carol and kept the shovel.

They crept toward the cottage and tried to peek in the windows, but all of them had shades pulled down or curtains closed. They stood on the porch looking at each other. Carol nodded and Sarah opened the door. It slid open easily.

Sarah walked in with Carol on her heels. Roydon was tied to a bed with duct tape over his mouth. A scene ripped right from the book *Misery*. But a wide-eyed Roydon shook his head and tilted it frantically toward a closed door.

Sarah whispered to Carol. "Go outside. Call 9-1-1."

Carol took out her phone. "No signal."

Sarah looked at her phone. She didn't have one either. "Go back up the road until you get a signal. Take the truck if you have to."

As Carol left, Sarah tiptoed over to the door. She put her ear against it, but didn't hear anything through the thick planks. Sarah glanced back at Roydon. He nodded. Go on, he seemed to be saying. Sarah slowly twisted the knob, her palm a bit damp. *Now or never.* Sarah flung the door open.

The nanny was out cold. Tied to the cast iron headboard of another bed.

Sarah froze in the doorway, looking back and forth between the nanny and Roydon. The nanny couldn't have tied Roydon up and then herself. Someone else did this, but who? Sarah decided to free Roydon, since at least he was awake. He could explain what the heck was going on and help her with the nanny. Sarah hadn't taken two steps when the front door of the cabin banged against the wall. Carol was shoved in, and Ella Mae followed her. Holding a gun. She looped an arm casually around Carol's neck.

"Why'd you have to come here and snoop around," Ella Mae said. "You've complicated my life."

"I don't think we're the ones who complicated it." The shovel Sarah held felt as useless as a feather. "Looks like you've done a fine job of that yourself, kidnapping the nanny and Roydon." Ella Mae was delusional if she thought Roydon would fall in love with her.

"Why?" Carol asked.

"Because Roydon and me were meant to be. Hey, that sounds like one of those stupid songs June Baby writes." Ella Mae lowered the gun to her side. "But I bided my time waiting for the perfect moment to make sure Roydon and I could get away together without anyone figuring it out."

"You thought if you waited long enough, Roydon would just go with you?" Sarah asked.

Ella Mae nodded. "I told June Baby to leave you two out of this. That she didn't need you. But you turned up anyway. And I'm sorry to say, it ain't going to end well for either of you. The sheriff will think the nanny killed you both, along with Roydon."

Roydon made a squeaking sound.

"Now don't you worry Roydon honey, I'm not going to kill you. *If* you're a good boy. We'll just leave a bit of evidence around to make them think the nanny buried you before these two made their rescue attempt, and that she killed them and offed herself."

I noticed movement behind Ella Mae. June stood there with a baseball bat.

"Buckle," Sarah yelled at Carol hoping she'd remember the story Sarah had retold last night about Monterey Bay. Hoping Ella May wouldn't.

Carol plopped down like a hound dog on a hot day. June whacked Ella May's gun arm and then her head for good measure. Once Ella May dropped the gun and crumpled to the floor, Sarah ran over and picked up the gun.

Minutes later, Roydon was untied and Ella May was hog-tied. Carol went up the road to call for help. Everyone else helped the nanny.

Thirty minutes later they watched while the sheriff tucked a handcuffed Ella May into the back of a squad car and an ambulance transported the drugged nanny to the hospital. Roydon explained that Ella May had found out the nanny had faked her papers for the agency and started blackmailing her. She'd made the nanny put up the pictures over time and send the texts to the burner phone.

"How did you find us, June?" Sarah asked.

"I was a might suspicious when you asked to borrow Roydon's truck to run errands, so I followed you. When I got here and spotted Ella May's Cadillac, I knew something was wrong."

Roydon had his arm around June. "Might be the best day of my life," he said, kissing the top of June's head.

"You can kiss my head anytime," June said. "Hey, that sounds like a great country song."

KEEP YOUR FRIENDS CLOSE

MAGGIE KING

"'Keep your friends close, but your enemies closer.' I never knew that quote came from *The Godfather*." Meryl McKinney's words mingled with the chatter of the coffee shop as she held up a tattered paperback copy of the famous tome by Mario Puzo. "Did you know that, Kat?"

"Nope. Never read *The Godfather*. Or saw the movie." Kat Berenger rested her blue eyes on Meryl. "Now, about my proposal: do we have a deal?" Kat and Meryl had chosen a table by a window in Zorro's, a trendy spot in Richmond's historic Fan District.

"Oh, absolutely! I'll do anything to catch the scumbag who killed my best friend." Meryl's voice caught and she took a deep breath.

"And I intend to clear Kenny of suspicion. My baby brother would never have killed his wife." Kat tossed back her blond curls, setting her earrings jingling.

The two women sealed the deal with a handshake. Kat couldn't help noticing the difference between her hands and Meryl's: while Kat decorated each finger with a ring and her black lacquered nails sported leopard tips, Meryl, nails bitten to the quick, wore no rings.

Five days before, Vicki Berenger's husband Kenny had come home from a weeklong trip and couldn't find his wife. He had the fright of his life when he opened the shower door and found her—dead. Forensics found that Vicki's shampoo contained a lethal mixture of DMSO and strychnine. Since that day, Kenny Berenger found himself in the crosshairs of the Richmond Police Department.

"They always suspect the spouse, don't they?" Meryl asked.

Kat nodded as customers came and went, ordering their oversized coffees and pastries to go.

Meryl went on. "What's DMSO anyway?"

"A supplement. People use it for arthritis. Some of my clients get it at the health food store." Kat was a personal trainer at Max's gym. "DMSO opens up your pores and allows your skin to absorb other chemicals. Like strychnine."

"And where would someone get strychnine?"

"It's commonly used in rat poison."

Meryl closed her eyes, perhaps hoping to block the images her mind conjured.

"First things first," Kat said. "Let's get some coffee. Then we can plan our strategy for putting Vicki's killer behind bars."

"My treat." When Kat started to protest, Meryl stood and held up a hand. "You're being so kind and supportive. I'm glad you suggested teaming up to solve Vicki's murder. Running into you yesterday at Kenny's was the best thing that could have happened to me."

"I've been spending a lot of time with Kenny. He stayed with me until the police released the crime scene. By the way, he and I loved the corn casserole you brought."

"Thanks. I'm just dreading the funeral tomorrow." Meryl's voice caught again. "Well, what can I get you?"

"Just a skinny latte. I had breakfast at home."

As Meryl walked up to the counter, Kat thought that the woman looked like she'd fallen out of bed five minutes before—and had probably spent the night tossing and turning. Tangled, greasy strands of dark hair brushed her shoulders. She wore a wrinkled cotton blouse, capris, and flip-flops worn down at the heels. Hard to believe that Meryl had recently turned forty-five. She looked much older.

Zorro prepared its coffee in a large roaster that took pride of place by the front window. Kat looked up at the stamped ceiling and down at the original wood floor, now scuffed and worn. Banners from Southern colleges—University of Richmond, College of William and Mary, Virginia Tech, and Virginia Commonwealth University among them—covered the walls, along with relics of the past, such as a framed ad for vanilla milk shakes at ten cents. Bookcases held used books. Plants that looked wilted in the soaring heat of a Virginia summer lined window ledges.

Kat glanced at the few people sitting nearby. A stern-looking man with a military bearing was reading a copy of the *Richmond Times-Dispatch*. A woman with blue-tinted black hair and oversized red-framed glasses moved to a beat only she could hear through her earbuds. A man of about thirty-five sported a rumpled tee shirt and a baseball cap promoting the Richmond Flying Squirrels, a minor league baseball team. He winked at Kat. She winked back. Despite being fifty something, Kat still enjoyed flirting with men.

As Meryl turned from the counter, Kat got up to help her carry the coffee and a strawberry scone. At the table, Meryl split the scone with a knife and offered half to Kat.

"I lost my job on Monday," Meryl said.

"Oh, no. You lost a dear friend *and* your job? All in the same week?"

Meryl nodded, looking glum. "Yeah. Downsizing. Or so they say. I need to get a job fast. I have so many expenses. I had to take a second job a while back, but it doesn't pay well."

"Where's that?"

"Oh, um—Burger King."

Kat raised her eyebrows, noting Meryl's hesitation. Aloud, she said, "What did you do at the job you lost? Where was it?"

"The Heller Corporation. It's an association management firm downtown. And I... um, I did pretty much everything." Meryl smiled, showing the gap between her two front teeth. "I answered phones, filed, prepared bank deposits, helped the CEO and the membership specialist. I was there for six years."

Kat took a sip of her latte. "So you did everything, huh? And you said they're downsizing?"

"Right."

"And after you were there for six years." Kat shook her head. "That's so unfair. These companies have no loyalty anymore."

After a moment's pause, Kat said, "Now let's talk strategy for nailing Vicki's killer. I figure that between the two of us, we know everyone Vicki knew. I'm especially interested in the women in your book group. Hopefully they'll be at the funeral tomorrow, and you can question them afterwards at the lunch."

"How do I question them? I can't just go, 'By the way, did you kill Vicki?'"

Vicki had been Kat's sister-in-law for three years. "No, you have to be subtle. Cagey. You know these women. And you'd known Vicki since... when? Kindergarten?" When Meryl nodded, Kat added, "I never really knew her. She and Kenny no sooner met than they married."

"I told her not to rush into marriage. But she wouldn't listen."

Kat thought she heard an accusing tone in Meryl's words. Did the woman think that if Vicki had held off on marrying Kenny, she'd still be alive?

Ignoring Meryl's subtext, Kat said, "Back to your book group—you all met last Thursday at Vicki's house and the very next day Vicki is dead. One of them either did it or might know something."

Meryl looked doubtful. "Maybe we need to leave this to the police."

"The police are laser-focused on Kenny. A retired homicide detective from the Richmond Police lives next door to me and stays in close touch with his former colleagues. He won't tell me much—doesn't want to obstruct the investigation—but he does throw me tidbits. I probably shouldn't repeat what he says"—Kat lowered her voice and leaned forward—"but Vicki was depositing three thousand bucks a month into her son's college fund. In cash."

"You're kidding."

"Where would she get that kind of money? She wasn't even working, she was getting her MBA."

Meryl looked blank. "From Kenny?"

"But why cash?"

Meryl's eyes filled with tears. "I shouldn't say this…" she trailed off.

"Of course, you should say it!" Kat said.

A young woman with a froth of pink hair and sleeves of tattoos sat in an overstuffed chair, a book in one hand and a yellow highlighter in the other. She turned, frowning, and said, "Please keep it down."

Kat glared at the woman, but dropped her voice before saying to Meryl, "We want to find Vicki's killer and anything you know could help."

"Okay, okay." Meryl paused for a moment to collect herself. "When Vicki was in college, she—she was an escort for a while, and then later she switched to phone sex. Maybe she started doing *that* again."

"But why would she?"

"She made good money at it. And she wanted to send her son to a good school for pre-med."

"Kenny makes good money," Kat said. "He'd be glad to help out."

"She didn't want Kenny to feel obligated to send her son to school. She wanted her ex to do it, but he wouldn't come through. So she told Kenny that her father had set up a fund for his grandson."

Kat didn't respond. Instead she slanted a look at Meryl. "That explains the money, but not the murder. Do you think someone from the book group killed Vicki?"

"Well… rumor has it that Tina Wood was having an affair with Kenny. So maybe she did it."

"If they were having an affair, she definitely had a motive. But she has a hell of a nerve going to their house and socializing with Vicki."

"Yes, well…" Meryl spread her hands.

"Did Tina use the bathroom the other night? If so, she had an opportunity to doctor the shampoo."

"I have no idea. I'm pretty sure we all used the facilities at least once. It's not the kind of thing you really notice." Tears spilled down Meryl's cheeks.

"Okay, take a minute." Kat pressed a tissue into Meryl's hand. "I know this is very upsetting."

"But what about…" Meryl trailed off, clearly uncomfortable. "What about Kenny?"

Kat sighed. "What *about* Kenny? He didn't do it. He was out of town on business all last week and didn't get home until Friday, when he found Vicki. And he loved her."

"But he was having an affair!"

"You said that was a rumor."

"He could have added the poison to the shampoo before he went out of town."

Kat sighed again. "Do you know how often Vicki washed her hair?"

Meryl looked startled at Kat's unexpected question. "Every other day. I think."

"Okay, let's say that Kenny did add the poison before he went out of town. He left on a Sunday, right?"

Meryl nodded.

"That means Vicki would have used that shampoo at least twice, maybe three times, before Friday. So why wasn't she poisoned earlier in the week?"

"She said she had her hair cut and shampooed by her stylist last week. Plus she alternated shampoos a lot."

Meaning that Kenny could indeed have managed to switch shampoo bottles before leaving for his trip. Kat became even more determined to clear her brother.

"Okay," Kat held up her hand. "Let's consider the method the killer used: DMSO mixed with strychnine."

"You said earlier that someone could get DMSO at the health food store. And that strychnine is in rat poison." When Kat nodded, Meryl continued. "So, we just have to find someone with a rat problem who also had a motive to kill Vicki."

Kat laughed ruefully. "From what my cop friend tells me, rat problems in the city are more common than you might realize."

"I imagine an Internet search would tell anyone how to mix DMSO with strychnine."

"You're right. But Internet search histories can be traced."

"The killer read it in a book, maybe? Some author used the same method?"

"That's what I've been thinking," Kat said. "Do you know Hazel Rose?"

"No."

"Hazel's a romance writer, but she's started writing mysteries. She's also something of an amateur sleuth. She's on a trip right now or else she'd be solving this mystery. She told me about a book on poisons that she uses for reference. The Richmond Public Library has a copy of the book."

"Really?"

Kat sipped her coffee. "I went to the library and found the book. I asked the librarian about mysteries featuring poison and she suggested several, including *An Unbecoming Death* which included a scene that was identical to how Vicki died."

"So it looks like the killer got the idea from that story." Meryl looked thoughtful as she chewed her scone. "The book group members all read mysteries."

"The librarian said that someone else had recently requested the same book. She wouldn't tell me who. Of course, she probably doesn't even know. But if we showed her a picture of the women in your book group…" Kat looked at Meryl. "What do you think of that idea?"

Meryl shoved a too-big piece of scone in her mouth and swallowed the food with the help of her coffee. "I really don't feel comfortable questioning people who could be killers."

"Okay. Let's ask ourselves which of these women had a motive. Besides Tina Wood allegedly having an affair with Kenny."

"I don't know. We all went to school together. Vicki stole Carol Sarris's boyfriend in senior year."

"That was almost thirty years ago. You think Carol would kill Vicki now?" Kat sounded doubtful.

"No. Just saying."

"Did any of the folks in your group have rat problems? Not that one has to actually have a rat problem to get rat poison, but it's a place to start."

Meryl chewed one of her well-chewed nails. "Lots of people have rat problems in the city."

"You're right." Kat drained her latte. "You mentioned that Vicki had been a phone sex operator. So maybe she blackmailed one of her clients."

Meryl's face lit up with hope. "I bet that's what it was."

"Don't get all excited. If it was one of her clients, he—or she—would have to have been in Vicki's house and used the bathroom. It's pretty unlikely that Vicki would ply her trade as a sex worker in her home. Assuming she even was a sex worker."

"Yeah. I guess." Meryl looked distressed at such a promising possibility coming to naught.

"But blackmail? That's an interesting possibility." Kat gave Meryl a long look. "How about this scenario: Vicki found out that her dearest friend, her lifelong friend, was embezzling funds from her employer."

The little color in Meryl's face drained. "Embezzling? I never heard Vicki mention anyone embezzling."

"When you said you did 'everything' for the Heller Corporation, did that include bookkeeping?"

"Yeah, so. Why are you asking?"

Kat leaned forward. "I heard one hundred thousand dollars is missing from Heller's general fund."

"Who told you this? Your cop buddy?"

"The Heller Corporation's Membership Specialist also belongs to Max's Gym. According to her, you were fired for embezzling."

"That's Patty Oates. And she is lying."

"I know your mom has a lot of medical problems. I know you took a second job at a fast food restaurant for the extra money. I also know the restaurant is having a problem with rats."

"You read too many mysteries. Besides Burger King isn't having any such problem."

"Did Vicki figure out you were stealing? Was she blackmailing you?"

Meryl said nothing, folding her arms as her gaze shot daggers at Kat.

"Remember when I said that the librarian said someone else had recently requested *An Unbecoming Death*?"

Meryl still didn't respond. She sat, looking mutinous.

"She picked you out of a Facebook lineup."

Meryl rolled her eyes. "Oh, please."

"And the fast food place where you work is C.J.'s, not Burger King." Kat swiped at the screen on her phone and read, "Former and current employees claim there is a rodent infestation at C.J.'s, a popular fast food restaurant in Richmond."

"Okay, maybe C.J.'s *had* a problem. But that happened way before I started there."

"But they probably still had the poison stashed away."

Tears suddenly filled Meryl's eyes and streamed down her face. "My best friend was bleeding me dry all so she could send her idiot son to an expensive pre-med program. I pity the poor people who end up being his patients."

Kat sat back, but said nothing.

"It all started when I borrowed a small amount from Heller so my mom's insurance wouldn't cancel. I was going to pay it back. I confessed this to Vicki one night when we drank too much wine. She immediately started blackmailing me and I had to keep embezzling to pay her. A few weeks ago she upped her fee from three thousand to thirty-five hundred. I couldn't do it. My mom has a lot of medical expenses, and her insurance premiums skyrocketed and my brother cares more about his gambling than our mother. I realized Vicki was never, *ever*, going to stop."

"Unless you stopped her."

Meryl sighed. "Yes. I hate computers and the library had all the information I needed to poison Vicki."

"You did get the poisoning idea from *An Unbecoming Death*?"

Narrowing her eyes, Meryl said, "Yes."

Kat was sure the police would find Meryl's prints on the book. Leveling her gaze at Meryl, she asked, "So how did you do it?"

"Like you said, I stole some rat poison from work, found DMSO at a health food store, and a bottle of Vicki's favorite shampoo from another store. I only had to dump some of the shampoo out and add the other ingredients to the bottle. Then at book group I excused myself to go to the bathroom and switched the bottles. Child's play. Too bad I didn't get to see the gory results." The look of pure hatred on Meryl's face alarmed Kat.

Kat tapped the cover of *The Godfather*. "'Keep your friends close, and your enemies closer?'"

"Meryl McKinney, I'm arresting you for…" The man in the Flying Squirrels cap and tattered tee shirt flashed his Richmond Police Department badge and finished reading Meryl her Miranda rights. The woman with the blue-tinted hair and oversized red-framed glasses approached and handcuffed a shrieking, cursing Meryl.

"I'm Detective Thomas Fischella and this is my partner, Detective Stephanie Garcia. You are under arrest."

"I'm going to kill you," Meryl hurled at Kat as the detectives hauled her away.

Zorro's customers and employees froze in their places, not speaking, not moving, as if in a tableau.

Gathering her purse, Kat walked out into a steamy July day. As she started her Mustang and drove toward police headquarters to give her statement, she muttered, "Can't wait to get this frigging wire off."

UNBRIDLED

KRISTIN KISSKA

Wet gravel crunched under my tires as I approached the Low-country Equestrian Center from the old oak-tree-lined entrance. Though still early, horses already trotted around the training rings, and I even glimpsed a flash of a horse's tail as someone rode into the woods. Ah, I lived for Saturday mornings at the stables! It was the home of my pride and joy gelding—Baymont Blues, or as I affectionately called him, Bay.

Though the rain had finally tapered off, it didn't soften the edge of South Carolina's notorious spring humidity. I'd already swatted a couple mosquitos this morning. Outfitted in leather boots and breeches, I hauled my grooming bucket into the stable. Parker, the head trainer, had agreed to meet for a private session this morning to polish my dressage techniques.

The stable's residents greeted me with their chorus of neighs, meows, and a stray bird tweeting from the rafters. I inhaled the cocktail of leather, brass, and hay—the most intoxicating scent on the planet—then walked the length of the wide hallway.

"G'mornin, Mia. You're here early." I winked at Parker's daughter. The teen slid Bay's stall gate open and stroked his muzzle, keeping his nose out of the bag of carrots I'd brought. "Did you ride your bike?"

"Hey, Courtney. Nope. Dad dropped me off before running errands. I wanted to clean up this messy boy. Dad would kill me if he knew I'd ridden him through the mud." As Parker's daughter Mia brushed D'Artagnan, each swift stroke revealed more of his dappled coat. Though tethered only by a halter and rope, the eighteen-hand Irish draught horse behaved like a gentle giant in her expert care.

"Don't worry. I won't tell," I said.

The empty stall and a quick glance at my friend Gina's tack box showed her horse Spade's saddle, bridle and girth were gone.

Hardly the usual weekend routine for Gina who'd relocated from Virginia last autumn. "Gina got here early. Did you see her?"

Mia shook her head. "Maybe she's nervous about Tryon and already practicing." Next weekend, many of our stable's horses and riders would caravan to Tryon International Equestrian Center for the opening of their Spring Series. Bay and Spade were entered in the dressage and jumper events—this was my first time ever competing against Gina.

"Maybe." I noticed the teen's smile didn't quite reach her soulful dark eyes. Poor thing looked haggard. "Did homework keep you up late?"

"Final exams are in a couple weeks. Calculus is the worst." Mia nodded, perking up a bit. "Only one more year till college."

Studying into the wee hours was not how I spent my Friday nights when I was in high school. "Where do you want to go?"

"South Carolina. Mama studied there."

Almost two years ago, her mother had departed for a weekend with her college girlfriends in Charleston, but had never returned. She'd died in a hit and run car accident.

Forcing a smile, I said, "I didn't know that. Go, Gamecocks!" I leaned my weight against Bay's shoulder to move him to the far side of the stall so I could muck it. "Gina graduated from USC, too."

"She mentioned that two days ago."

"Really?"

"Gina recognized Mama from the photo I keep in my wallet. Turns out they were good friends in college. Gina hadn't realized Mama and I were related."

Brave girl, on so many levels. "Does Gina know..." Yikes, I didn't mean to remind her of her mother's death. It must be hard enough living with a new, moody stepmother who was a couple of weeks shy of giving birth to her half-brother. But I'd already ventured down this path, so I softened my voice and continued, "Hard to believe it's been almost two years since your mom died."

"Seventeen months. Three weeks. Two days." Mia paused combing D'Artagnan's mane and glanced away, exhaling before continuing. "Gina was there. In Charleston. When Mama died."

We both turned at the sound of footsteps approaching.

"Hey, have y'all seen Gina?" Scott, Gina's husband, asked. "Spade's stall is still empty. I'd call but she left her cell phone in the car when I dropped her off an hour ago. Didn't notice 'til I got home. Figured she'd need it."

"I can give it to her," I said.

"Thanks," Scott said.

I slipped it into the back pocket of my riding breeches as Scott strolled away.

Activity in the stable picked up as more horse owners arrived. Finally, I had Bay brushed, bridled, padded, and saddled. While I summoned every ounce of strength I could muster to tighten the buckle straps on Bay's girth, a large, dark shadow entered the far side of the stable and trotted toward us.

Spade's saddle was empty, his stirrups bounced drunkenly, and his broken rein scraped the brick floor. He slowed to a walk as he entered his stall, and then nipped at his hayrack, content to be home.

But no Gina.

Parker pulled up to the stables and parked as Mia and I raced outside.

"Hey, Parker! I think Spade threw Gina. Can you help me look for her around the grounds?"

"Sure." Concern overshadowed his Hollywood good looks. "Mia, you ride with me."

"Okay, Dad," Mia said.

Parker drove his pickup truck east as I drove my SUV west. Separate directions ensured we'd cover the equestrian center's collection of fields, paddocks, and riding rings faster. When I found no sign of Gina, I parked by the horse trailers near the arena near the lower grounds. I searched the trailers and then ran inside the covered arena. At every turn, I feared I would find her in a lump at the foot of some jump.

But there was no sign of Gina—injured or otherwise.

I got back in my SUV and drove until I pulled up alongside Parker's truck. I opened my window. Grasping for ideas, I ventured, "Someone rode into the trails as I arrived early this morning. It could have been Gina."

"Worth a look," Parker said.

"I'll return to the stable in case Gina returns," Mia said. "Dad, text me if you find her."

Parker patted his pockets, and then shrugged. "Must've forgotten my phone."

Mia shook her head. "Courtney, can you text me?"

"I sure can. Be careful," I said.

Mia's brow couldn't have been more furrowed as she hopped out of her father's truck and jogged back to the stable. Poor thing. This had to remind Mia of the last day she kissed her mother goodbye.

"Don't worry, y'all," I said. "I bet we'll laugh over our search-and-rescue misadventures later."

"Let's hope," Parker said.

When we reached the fork, I drove down Gina's and my favorite trail—the one that leads to a large meadow with a creek. Parker searched the other. I made it about a mile into the trail before the trees became too close for my SUV to pass. I'd have to walk—or rather, slog through the mud—the rest of the way.

Lordy, what could've possessed Gina? We horse owners are quite a superstitious bunch. Even under good conditions, no one would ride a trail before competing in a show. This ground was so saturated; she risked Spade going lame with a sprained ankle.

After a few turns along the path, I spotted a purple helmet lying in the mud. And a body, sprawled nearby. Oh, no.

"Gina!" I called out, but no response. No hint of movement.

Adrenaline flooded my veins as I rushed to her, then felt for a pulse, careful not to move her. She was breathing. Her arm lay at an unnatural angle.

Grooves of mud from where Spade had skidded filled with standing water. Thank God she hadn't landed face down in a puddle. And why on earth would someone leave loose nails lying on the ground? A horse could've injured his hooves. Or thrown his rider.

After calling 9-1-1, I texted Scott and Mia: Found Gina unconscious. Meet us at hospital.

* * * *

Scott paced the hospital's lounge while the rest of us tried to remain optimistic and supportive. Gina had still not awakened by the time she was admitted to the emergency room. The piped-in instrumental music kept my nerves on edge.

Parker's wife, Jane—with dark circles under her eyes and rumpled maternity clothes—navigated the tight cluster of chairs with a hand on her swollen belly and a bag of sandwiches in the other. She looked ready to check into the hospital herself.

"How's Gina, bless her heart?" Jane hugged Scott.

"We're still waiting," Scott said.

Jane shoved the bag of sandwiches at Mia. "Pass these around."

Mia took the sandwiches, but I was annoyed. Not so much as a please or thank you, which in my mind nullified any goodwill Jane just earned from bringing lunch. Ever the Southern gentleman, Parker helped his daughter unpack the sandwiches.

"No word from the surgeon yet. Still hangin' on by a prayer." Scott twisted his wedding ring. "She has to pull through. Gina's my everything."

For a hot minute, I was jealous that Gina had a spouse whose existence depended on her recovery. Who besides my parents would pace the floor for me had I been critically injured? Then again, every dollar and free minute I could muster went into boarding, riding, and keeping Bay in oats. But at thirty-something, I'd yet to meet anyone who could tempt me from my equestrian lifestyle.

"Parker-sugar, I'm going home for a nap. Please keep me posted." Jane waddled toward the exit. But before she reached the door, she turned to glare at me. "Gotta take care of *all* of Parker's girls, right, Courtney?"

Holy hell! Heat radiated up my neck. What was Jane insinuating? That Parker was having an affair? Certainly, not with me or with Gina, either. I bit my cheek to keep from sassing her.

Parker and Jane had enjoyed a whirlwind romance and married less than a year later. As far as I could tell, their lives were perfect. Why would Jane be jealous?

Just then, Gina's surgeon, dressed in light blue scrubs and cap, arrived. Mia slipped over to her dad, clinging to his side.

Despite the doctor's tired smile, Scott's face drained to a clammy shade of pale. "Your wife's in the recovery room. She did well. We had to set her arm with pins, and she has two broken ribs, but no signs of spinal injury. Scans showed minimal brain swelling. We'll keep her for a few days to monitor her, but I'm optimistic."

"Oh, thank God." Scott pumped the doctor's hand like he'd won a blue ribbon at the state championships. "When can I see her?"

"The nurse will escort you back in a bit." He pulled Scott aside and lowered his voice for a measure of privacy. I pretended to collect my car keys to eavesdrop unnoticed. "Gina has severe contusions across her collarbone and left shoulder."

"She was horseback riding," Scott said. "Her horse returned with the reins broken. Spade must've spooked and thrown her. Could that have caused her injuries?"

"Doubt it. Probably something thin, like a wire or rope of some sort. Two inches higher and… well, she was very lucky."

Since the rest of us wouldn't be allowed to see her with Scott, we all expressed our relief along with get-well-soon sentiments and departed. Knowing my friend would recover, I planned to spend the afternoon working with Bay. I offered to drop Mia at home before returning to the stables since Parker had lessons scheduled all afternoon.

As Mia and I walked to the parking lot, Gina's cell phone vibrated in my back pocket. In the excitement, I'd forgotten I still had it.

"Hang tight a minute, sweetie." I dashed back inside the hospital to return the phone to Scott.

While I rode the elevator, a new message flashed in from Gina's out-of-town sister. Planning to reply with an update on Gina's condition, I noticed several unread text messages. But her exchange with Parker yesterday caught my eye.

Gina: I need to see you. Privately.

Parker: Meet me at the trail ride's meadow tomorrow at 7 am.

My gut twisted in the same way it had when I found Gina a crumpled mess this morning. I couldn't believe what I was reading. A secret tryst? Maybe Jane had been on to something.

Were Gina and Parker having an affair?

I hung onto the phone and returned to the car where Mia was waiting. Getting Mia to talk on the way home was like coaxing Bay to take his medications without the mint paste. Since she was staring out her window, I couldn't see her face, but she kept wringing her hands.

"You were at school yesterday, right?" I asked.

Mia nodded.

"What was your dad up to?"

"He bought a new horse trailer for this show season."

"And your stepmom?"

"Some work conference."

"When did Jane get home?"

"Eight or so last night."

"Is that normal for her?" I don't know how much Parker made as the Lowcountry Equestrian Center's head trainer, but I gathered that Jane, as a corporation lawyer, was the family breadwinner. Jane's job also meant late hours and travel.

Mia shrugged.

"Was Jane in a sour mood?" Nothing like nine months of pregnancy hormones to fuel jealousy and maybe even plot a little revenge.

"I try to stay out of her way. I'm either in my bedroom studying or at the stables where I can hang out with Dad by himself."

"Why?"

"Jane made it pretty clear I was a burden. She'd be happier if I weren't around. Especially once the baby is born."

"Oh, Mia-sweetie, Jane respects your relationship with your dad. He's your only living parent."

"I overheard Jane and Dad arguing the other night. As much she wants me to move out of the house tomorrow, she doesn't want to pay my college tuition. The weird thing is, she already opened a college savings account for the baby."

"Don't give up. I'm sure your dad has been saving for your education. Plus, you can apply for scholarships. And student loans. You could work and save money—"

"I wish Mama were alive, then I wouldn't have to deal with Jane." The tear snaking down her cheek almost caused me to drive into the ditch.

Oh, the rotten hand of cards this sweet child had been dealt! This beautiful raven-haired girl, whose dark eyes were strikingly similar to her mother's, who had lost her mother in a hit-and-run car accident only to be introduced to her replacement less than a year later. And now on track for demotion to second-class kid once her half-brother was born.

"Hang in there, sweetie. I'm always here if you need to talk." I pulled into the driveway to drop her off. Rather than let her walk into Jane's territory distraught, I leaned over to hug her. "Your dad is so proud of you, and your mom would've been too."

"Thanks." She wiped her cheeks before entering the house.

Instead of immediately returning to the stables, I stopped by the tack store to pick up a bag of feed for Bay. Besides, I craved the few extra minutes to sort through the tornado of thoughts swirling in my head.

Gina was an experienced, ribbon-winning rider. She'd never have willingly risked riding Spade through muddy conditions were it not important. Something made her override her caution.

The surgeon suspected her fall hadn't been an accident, and that it could've killed her. Who would want to murder Gina? Was it so-pregnant-she-was-ready-to-pop Jane? Or maybe her alleged lover Parker lured her?

Gina had sent the first text. I had a hard time believing Gina would cheat on Scott, but the text proved she was determined to meet Parker privately. Then again, Scott had Gina's cell phone this morning. Perhaps he intercepted their text exchange and tried to stop to their rendezvous. Maybe he thought Parker would be riding the trail. Jealousy could cause good people to do dark deeds.

Pushing a wheelbarrow with Bay's oats up the stable's central hall toward his stall, I craned to look for Parker, then remembered he was teaching lessons all afternoon.

D'Artagnan's stall was empty except for a muddy bicycle leaning against the wall. Stuffed behind the water trough was a plastic shopping bag—hardly a safe item to keep near a horse's stall. But when I grabbed the bag, a receipt for wire and flat head nails slipped out. Purchased yesterday afternoon. And I'd seen loose nails near Gina's fall.

Oh, sweet Jesus. Spade hadn't thrown her after all.

In all the chaos of searching for Gina earlier this morning and getting her to the hospital, I'd broken one of my strict personal rules—I'd left Bay in his stall fully tacked with his saddle and bridle on. But that would help me now. After calling 9-1-1, I gave instructions to the stable hand where to send the police. Within minutes I led Bay outside, mounted him, and cantered toward the woods.

But once we entered the trail, I tightened the reins to slow him to a controlled trot. I couldn't risk him going lame on some divot or root hidden by mud and water. When I approached the place where I'd abandoned my SUV this morning to search on foot, I decelerated Bay to a walk and leaned against his neck, protecting my own.

Bay followed the trail around a bend hidden by a hill. I spotted D'Artagnan standing in the distance while his rider Mia used a hammer to remove a nail from high up a tree. I halted Bay, snapped a photo, and then typed Parker's number in my cell phone. Then I hit *send* to place the call.

A ringtone sounded from Mia's back pocket. She stopped coiling a thin wire still attached to a tree on the opposite side of the trail and glanced back at me.

Busted.

"Mia-sweetie, what were you thinking? You could've killed Gina this morning." I nudged Bay forward with my knees.

Mia's forehead crinkled beneath her riding helmet. All color drained from her face. "Stop, Courtney. Don't come any closer!"

"Okay." Tightening Bay's reins, we halted a healthy distance away. I couldn't let Mia bolt. D'Artagnan could beat Bay in a race any day. "You've had your dad's cell phone the whole time, haven't you? Let me guess, you saw Gina's text and assumed they were having an affair, so you lured her to the riding trail."

"It wouldn't have been the first time he cheated, but no. Dad's devoted to Jane." After coiling the wire, Mia used her hammer to pull a nail from the same tree where I'd found loose nails—carelessly dropped earlier, no doubt.

Coughing to mask my sigh of relief—I couldn't imagine Gina stooping to seduce a married man, or any man for that matter—I pressed on to keep Mia talking.

"Then what did Gina need to tell your Dad privately that would make you try to ki—hurt her?" I kept my voice soft so as not to spook her.

"I didn't mean to hurt her." Tears brewed in her eyes, then spilled down her cheeks. "It was an accident. A terrible mistake."

"No, Mia. Stringing wire up and then pretending to be your dad was intentional."

"Not Gina. *Mama.*" A cloud, as stormy as the ones hovering overhead, soured Mia's features. But then her groan launched a small flock of birds nearby. "I never meant to hurt her."

"I don't understand." My gut twisted. Her mother had been killed in a hit and run accident, but the police never found the driver. But then a new theory sent my mind whirling. "Wait. Were you the driver?"

She nodded, hiccupping between sobs. "About an hour after Mama left with her college friends for their girls' weekend, I found Dad and Jane together. Like, *together* together. I tried to call Mama, but she didn't answer her phone. I had to warn her. So, I took Dad's car and drove to Charleston. Oh, why didn't she just answer her cell phone? None of this would've ever happened."

"But you weren't old enough to have a driver's license then."

"No. Just my learner's permit. I knew where she and her friends were staying. Mama was furious when saw me drive up alone, so she ran out into the street to stop me. But I was so upset. So nervous. I got confused and jammed on the gas pedal instead of the brakes and I…"

"You hit her." Oh, such a burden of guilt this girl carried. My heart broke for her, and yet, her reality had brutal, life-shattering implications. "Why did you leave the scene?"

"I was so scared I kept driving. I knew Mama's college friends would call an ambulance to help her. I thought she'd be okay. But she wasn't. I never told anyone. I didn't know what would happen if I did. Would I go to jail? Would Dad hate me?" Her eyes pleaded with me, but for what? Understanding? Forgiveness? "I couldn't lose him, too. After Mama died, Dad was all I had left."

"What did you do with your father's car?"

"I drove it into the garage door."

I'd forgotten about her car accident. She'd sworn she'd just been trying to back out of the driveway and accidently shifted into drive. "You kept a big secret all this time."

"After Mama's funeral, Dad and Jane got married. I wasn't even invited." Mia wiped her face on her forearm, still holding the hammer. "Since the police never linked my car accident to Mom's death, I figured it was all over. Case closed. My secret lay buried in Mama's grave, until…"

"Until two days ago, when Gina saw the photo of you and your mother." In my peripheral vision, police officers crept around the bend positioning themselves in the trees.

"She was there when Mama died."

"She realized you were the hit and run driver, didn't she?"

"That *stupid* picture in my wallet." Mia squeezed her eyes shut, her face twisted in agony. She loved that photo, as it was the last one ever taken of her mom with her. She always carried it. "Gina threatened to have the police reopen the case."

"So you tried to stop Gina before she could tell Parker."

"Please, Courtney. Don't tell him. Don't tell my daddy." Her raspy voice hitched on the one word that belied this young adult's youth. Her naiveté.

"I'm so sorry, sweetie, but the authorities need to know." Each word uttered ripped my heart to shreds, yet reinforced my resolve. Mia was in over her head. I'd promised to help her. To be there for her. And I would. Every step of her brutal journey. But first, this young woman needed to own up to the mistakes she'd made. "Parker will understand. Over time—Oh!"

"No!" Mia jammed her heels into D'Artagnan's side, sending him charging toward me at full gallop.

Before I could steer Bay out of the way, a cop lunged from a nearby tree as Mia passed under, landing on D'Artagnan's rump and taking control of both horse and rider.

Less than an hour later, a fleet of blue strobe lights pulsed through the woods in the waning dusk. Mia's wrists were handcuffed, and the police had cordoned off the trail with yellow tape. As I finished giving my statement to one of the officers, Scott and Parker hopped out of an arriving squad car.

"Mia?" With a stony face, Parker raced past us to his daughter and D'Artagnan. "What's going on?"

Scott took Bay's reins from me to escort us back to the stables. Once we were out of earshot, he asked, "Are you okay, Courtney? Did Mia hurt you?"

"Still in shock, but I'm fine." Bay nudged my shoulder with his muzzle. "How's Gina?"

"She woke up and spoke with me for a couple minutes. Hopefully, she'll be back in the saddle before autumn."

"Thank God." I hugged Scott.

"What the hell got into Mia? Dang, that girl came unglued."

I stopped and looked back in the distance at the precious-yet-broken girl, wrists tethered behind her, pleading with her dad. My gut sank to somewhere around my knees at the thought of the dark secret he was learning. Poor guy.

"Unglued? More like unbridled."

DEADLY DEVONSHIRE

SAMANTHA MCGRAW

"What do you mean Kate's dead? She can't be. Check again." Tess glanced up from the scattered contents of the woman's handbag, now strewn around her on the floor.

"Sorry, Tess," replied her assistant Jonah. "I hate to say this, but she's gone."

Just minutes earlier, Kate Pullman was enjoying her lunch at The Tea Cottage. Everyone knew Kate had a nut allergy, but she always carried an EpiPen and was so careful about what she ate.

But without warning, Kate had reached for her purse as she started to wheeze. Tess had rushed to help her, dumping the purse out on the floor and frantically tossing its contents about, but the pen wasn't there. Tess had called out to everyone in the teahouse asking if anyone had an EpiPen, but no one did. They all rushed over, circling around as Kate crumpled to the base of her chair.

Tess had tried to open Kate's airway, but it was too late. Kate was dead.

Now, Tess and all the patrons in the tearoom were in shock, stunned that a seemingly healthy young woman had died right before their eyes. Some were holding hands; others had tears streaming down their faces.

"Tess," whispered Daniel Rosen, one of the tearoom regulars, "I just got off the phone with 9-1-1. The dispatcher said the police and rescue can't get here right away. The temperatures have dropped faster than anyone expected. Those snow flurries outside have turned to sleet, and the roads have iced over. Every available cop and ambulance is on a call. Since North Carolina hardly ever gets snow, they aren't prepared. She has no idea how long it will take help to arrive."

"What?" Tess took a deep breath, aware everyone was watching. Then whispering to Daniel, "You mean nobody's coming?"

"Not right this minute. The dispatcher asked everyone to remain at the tearoom until they arrived."

"Hell's bells! I can't believe this is happening!" Tess said.

"What are we going to do?" Jonah helped Tess stand.

"Let me think," she said.

A dead customer was the last thing The Tea Cottage needed. Tess had sunk her life savings into the charming building. It had been built in the early 1900s and originally served as the town pharmacy. The pharmacist and his family used to live in the two-room apartment upstairs, but her assistant Jonah lived there now.

Tess decided from the beginning to maintain the building's historical charm. She spent hours polishing the original hardwood floors, oiling the mahogany counter and repainting the open shelves. She hired a glass company to restore the stained-glass windows to their original condition. Once the antique dining tables and chairs had been put in place, she fashioned a small reading nook in the front corner with two soft armchairs and a variety of books to please any reader.

Tess had worked so hard to make her business cozy and warm, a place where her guests could escape the outside world for least for an hour or two. And her guests loved spending time here so much that many came several times a week.

And now, one of her regulars had died.

Right in the dining room!

This news would soon spread through their little town of Havenport, North Carolina, faster than chicken pox in a kindergarten classroom. Some of her guests were already murmuring to each other, asking for their checks and even reaching for their coats.

"Everyone," Tess said. "Please go back to your seats and wait for the police to arrive. It shouldn't be long."

No one moved.

"I understand you want to leave. I know seeing Kate like this must be very frightening, and the weather is getting worse," Tess said. "But the police are going to need to talk to all of you, so they can figure out what happened to Kate."

Several guests nodded, others didn't look convinced.

"I promise Jonah and I'll make sure y'all get home safe." And then to ease their concerns about the drive home, "Jonah grew up in Vermont and lived there until last year. This kind of weather is normal for him. He will be happy to drive each and every one of you home in our delivery truck if he has to, right, Jonah?"

"Yes," Jonah said. "Of course."

"So please, be patient. Only a little while longer."

As the guests returned to their tables, Tess grabbed two fresh tablecloths from the kitchen and covered Kate's body. Next, she removed food-safe gloves from her apron and tugged them on. She needed to understand what had happened, which meant she might have to touch things she knew she shouldn't.

Trying to settle her nerves, she thought through the last hour. "Jonah, I'm sure I didn't make anything with nuts this morning. Did you?"

"No, nothing," he said. "I didn't even take nuts out of the pantry. None of today's recipes called for them."

"So how did she have an allergic reaction? We need to check her food."

Tess eyeballed every dish on the table without touching anything at first, but when she got to the Devonshire cream, she noticed a shiny coating on the top that she didn't recognize. By the looks of it, Kate had dipped into it and spread some on her scone. She held the small dish up to the light and then sniffed it.

"Almonds!" She whispered to Jonah. "Someone put almond extract on top of this Devonshire!"

"If that's the case, that means this was intentional," he whispered. "Put it down, the police will need it for evidence."

"Someone in our shop killed Kate," she said.

"Who here knew her?" he asked.

"Kate worked for Phyllis Ingram's husband, Marcus. She was here alone one table away waiting for a friend. Rose Landry was two tables away. Kate lived next door to Rose at the Bed & Breakfast. And Kate told me she went out with Daniel Rosen a few times. But I wouldn't think any of them had a reason to kill her."

"Well, somebody did, and if we don't figure it out soon, they might destroy any evidence they have on them before the police arrive. We need to talk to those three. Who do you think we should start with?"

"Daniel Rosen. Why don't you ask him to come back over here? Be discreet; we don't want to alarm anyone."

"Sure."

"And Jonah, we should save all the food in the kitchen in case the police need it. Would you mind packing everything up while I talk to Daniel?" Tess asked.

"Sure, I'll be in the back if you need me."

A moment later, Tess and Daniel were sitting together at an empty table in the back of The Tea Cottage dining room while the rest of the guests whispered among themselves near the front picture window. "Daniel, I'm trying to figure out what happened to

Kate, so I want to talk to the people who knew her. She once told me that the two of you were seeing each other. Is that right?"

"Yeah, but not for long. We only went out a few times before she called it quits."

"Why did she end it?"

"She said we didn't have much in common, but I got the feeling she was seeing someone else. Before our last date, she'd canceled on me a couple of times saying she had to work late. But I passed her office on my way home, and it was dark. She definitely wasn't working. At least, not in the office."

"Did you have any resentment towards her for the breakup?"

"No, not at all. We stayed friendly. I mean, we didn't talk much anymore, and we never went out again, but she was always nice when we ran into each other. I saw her when I came in for lunch today and went over to say hi. We chatted for a few minutes."

"About what?"

"You know, the usual stuff. How's work, nice weather, that kinda thing," Daniel answered.

Tess sensed there was something he wasn't telling her. "Can you think of anyone who might want to hurt Kate?"

"Wait, what? Are you saying someone did this to her on purpose?"

"It looks that way. Did she ever mention having trouble with anyone?" Tess asked.

"Kate? No! Of course not. She's as nice as they come. Everyone liked her. I can't believe anyone would want to hurt her."

"Thanks, Daniel. I appreciate you talking to me. Remember, don't leave until the police arrive."

"Sure." Daniel looked down at the white tablecloth covering Kate's body before slipping back to join the rest of the guests.

Tess wasn't sure if she saw sadness or remorse in his eyes.

"What'd you think, Tess?" Jonah asked as he came out from the kitchen. "I heard him say he spoke to Kate when he came in today. Do you remember seeing him?"

"I was so busy, but I think so. If he did, I'm sure it must have been polite because there weren't any raised voices, and she never looked tense or upset. But she did break up with him. He might be lying about them still being friendly. I want to find out if Phyllis knows anything. I know she stops by her husband's office frequently, maybe she's seen or heard something there."

Gently touching Phyllis on the arm, she whispered "Can I have a word with you? In the back, where we can have some privacy, if you don't mind."

"Sure, I suppose," Phyllis responded.

The two walked toward the back, and as they sat down, Tess bumped the table, knocking a teacup to the floor and spilling its contents. The porcelain shattered in a dozen pieces and the tea splashed around Phyllis's Kate Spade bag.

"Oh, Phyllis, I'm so sorry. It looks like I spilled some tea on your purse. Let me get a towel."

"Don't worry about it, dear," Phyllis said. "I'm forever setting my purse down where I shouldn't. I got that spot a couple of days ago when I set my purse on the floor at another restaurant. I haven't had a chance to clean it."

"Oh, I'm just glad I didn't do that. I'd be upset if I ruined your beautiful bag." Tess picked up the sharp broken teacup before anyone could cut themselves. "I wanted to ask you something. I saw you talking to Kate today. Do you know if anything was bothering her?"

"No, I don't think so. Everything seemed fine. I saw her over at the office earlier when I took Marcus his lunch. When I saw Kate, I mentioned that I was meeting a friend from Wilmington here for lunch, and she said lunch here sounded like a good idea. I ran a couple of errands and arrived a little before my friend. Anyway, Kate was already having lunch when I sat down. I stopped by her table for a minute to see what she had ordered. We spoke for a few minutes, and then I went to my own table. You had just served my tea when my friend texted and said she wouldn't be able to make it because of the snow. I guess she was right."

"I'm sure Marcus shares things with you. Did he mention if Kate was having a problem with anyone? Were there any issues you or he were aware of?"

"Are you saying this wasn't an accident?" Phyllis gasped and her hand flew to her chest.

"It looks like someone did this on purpose. I'm trying to figure out what happened in case anyone else might be in danger."

"Oh dear! I can't imagine anyone wanting to hurt Kate."

"What else can you tell me about her?"

"Well, I know she moved here about two years ago from somewhere up north, I don't remember where. She started working for Marcus shortly after that. She didn't date much and the poor girl couldn't have had much of a social life because she and Marcus were always working late," Phyllis said. "I know she bought that adorable stone cottage next door to Rose Landry's B&B. She often talked about working in her garden on her days off. I think she led a pretty quiet life."

"Daniel mentioned that they dated for a bit, but had recently broken up. He thought Kate was seeing someone new. Do you know who it might've been?"

"No, I can't say that I do," Phyllis replied. "She hasn't mentioned anyone to me. And between us girls, I don't think her relationship with Daniel ended well. Marcus said he was calling the office several times a day, bothering her after they broke up. He heard Kate arguing with him on the phone at least once."

"Really? That's good to know. Thanks for your patience. The police should be here soon, and hopefully, we'll all be able to get home without much trouble."

Tess glanced out the display window where all the guests, including Daniel and Phyllis, were gathered. The sleet was still coming down hard. She wondered how much longer it might take for the police and ambulance to get there.

She decided she needed to speak to elderly Rose Landry. Her Bed & Breakfast was next door to Kate's house, and she was just nosy enough to watch who was coming and going.

"Thank you for being so patient, Mrs. Landry," she said as they sat down at a table away from everyone else. "I know you want to get home, especially in this weather. I promise, as soon as the police are done with us, I'll have Jonah make sure you get home safe and sound. While we're waiting though, I wanted to ask whether you had noticed any trouble at Kate's house. Anyone bothering her?"

"No, I haven't seen anything unusual," Mrs. Landry said. "Well, except for a couple of nights ago. I did notice someone leaving pretty late when I was looking out the kitchen window. But it was dark, and I couldn't make out who it was. It looked like a man, though. She seemed fine, happy. Actually, happier than usual the past couple of weeks. I don't know why, she never said."

"Was she a good neighbor? Did y'all get along okay?"

"Oh yes, she was delightful. We had a problem when she first moved in, but that's all taken care of now."

"Really? What happened?"

"She was planting a garden and fixing up her backyard when she dug up a hydrangea bush on the property line. It was mine. I was quite upset about it. I'd had that bush for a long time, but she apologized and took it right down to the nursery to see if it could be saved. Fortunately, the roots were mostly intact, so someone from the nursery was able to replant it. She even paid for him to come back a few times to check and make sure it was growing strong again. She felt terrible about it."

"Thank you, Mrs. Landry. I'm sure the police will be here soon, and we'll all be able to go home. Until then, Jonah and I will get everyone some more tea while we wait."

"Thank you, dear, that would be lovely." Mrs. Landry wobbled back to the rest of the group.

Tess went to talk to Jonah. "Let's get everybody some fresh tea and maybe a few sandwiches while we wait for the police. Some of our guests hadn't had lunch yet when this happened, and you know I don't like for anyone go hungry. I was raised with better manners than that."

"Sure. Is everything okay? Was anyone able to tell you anything?" Jonah asked.

"Something's bothering me," Tess replied. "I'm not sure what, but I'll figure it out."

Jonah nodded. "In the meantime, I'll get the hot water and put together a couple of plates of sandwiches."

"I'll pass the tea box so our guests can decide what they'd like."

As Tess started to walk behind the counter for the tea box, Phyllis's purse caught her eye. She noticed the stain Phyllis said was a few days old. It wasn't faded but looked fresh. How could it be fresh?

In a flash, Tess understood.

She knew who killed Kate and why.

Leaving the tea box behind, she walked over the guests gathered together near the window.

"Phyllis, you said you took Marcus his lunch today, right? At his office?"

"Yes, why?"

"And you spoke to Kate while you were there. You mentioned coming here for lunch and suggested she do the same, am I right?"

Phyllis stiffened. "Well, yes, but I don't see what that has to do with anything."

"It has everything to do with what happened to Kate. If I'm right, you saw your opportunity this morning."

"I don't understand, Dear."

"You slipped Kate's EpiPen out of her purse while you were at the office. Everyone knew where she kept it so it would have been easy. Then, you planted the idea for her to come here for lunch, when you mentioned you were meeting a friend here. But you never planned on meeting anyone here."

"I don't know what you are talking about?" Phyllis said tensely.

"You wanted to get near Kate while she was eating. I'm guessing that you distracted her for a minute and poured almond extract over the Devonshire cream."

"That's crazy!" Phyllis looked to the other patrons and then laughed as if this was a bad joke. "Why would I do something like that? Kate was a sweet girl, I had no reason to hurt her," she argued.

"Considering all the late nights at work, I'm guessing there wasn't much actual work going on when she was with your husband Marcus. Daniel said it was dark when he drove by Kate's office, which makes me think Kate and Marcus were holed up somewhere else. That's why she broke up with Daniel and why Ms. Landry said she'd been so happy lately. Am I right?"

"No, you are not!"

Tess grabbed Phyllis's purse off the floor and sniffed the stain. "This spot isn't from putting it on the floor. It smells like almond extract. You were in such a hurry, you didn't put the cap back on tight, and it leaked everywhere."

Phyllis burst into tears. "My stupid jerk of a husband! How could he have an affair with that tramp, after all I've done for him? He was going to leave me for her! I found the divorce papers in his office, and I knew I had to do something to keep him from her."

Just then the front doorbells jingled, and a police officer walked in. "Hey y'all, sorry for the delay. I got here as quick as I could. The ambulance shouldn't be too far behind. Who wants to tell me what happened?"

As if rehearsed, everyone turned in unison and looked at Tess.

"I guess that would be me," Tess said.

BURN

K.L. MURPHY

"You called 9-1-1," Greg said.

Lillian Parker pursed her lips. "Was that a question?"

The wooden chair creaked under his weight. "I guess not."

She peered at him over her glasses. He was the fire chief now, grayer and heavier than when she'd taught him in high school but still the same—easily led, eager to please. "That's what I thought."

He lowered his chin, the flesh bulging over the collar of his starched shirt. "The 9-1-1 call came in just after 3 am."

"I know what time it was, Greggie."

"It's Greg now." Silent, Lillian shrugged and sipped her tea. "Three in the morning is pretty late to be awake, if you don't mind me saying."

Lillian was often awake during the night, rising when the throbbing pain came. It happened more often now, but he didn't need to know that. "I do mind." She smiled. "Greg."

He rubbed his large hands against his thighs. His nails were bitten to the quick, the skin around them red and ragged. "The house was owned by Trudy Trimble. Do you know her?"

"Of course, I know her. Being old does not make me stupid."

"I didn't say—"

She cut him off. "Trudy Trimble is her married name, but she'll always be Trudy Horning to me. Carter Horning was her grand-daddy. You might remember him. He and my daddy built these houses together." Both houses, splintered and worn by decades of wind and salt and sea, had been standing longer than Lillian had been alive. How many times had she wandered down to the beach as a girl and seen the two men standing knee deep in the sea, fishing rods in their hands, heads thrown back in laughter? She shook away the memory. "Trudy's grandmother—that was Millie Horning—we were best friends when we were girls. Stayed close all our lives, too. Even after she passed, the Horning family kept coming." She paused. "Trudy's like a granddaughter to me."

Greg's head bobbed. "I remember the Hornings. Brent and I got to be pretty good friends one summer when we worked at that sandwich shop on Main, the one next to the Stop 'n' Go Shop."

"Ben McCardle's place."

"Right. I think it's a Chipotle now."

Lillian set her cup on the side table. Ben McCardle had made the best pimento cheese in the county, maybe even the whole state of South Carolina. His grilled pimento cheese and bacon sandwiches had been famous for a while, but that was before the heart attack and the medical bills. There'd been at least a dozen places there since Ben had been forced to pull up stakes. She didn't know what a Chipotle was and figured she never would, but she did miss those sandwiches.

"Brent is Trudy's daddy. He lives in Atlanta now," she said. "He gave the house to Trudy as a wedding present." Her gaze drifted to the window, to the black shell that had been the Horning house. Dark wisps of smoke curled up and faded into the gray sky. The fire had been extinguished—their expression, not hers—yet the air still smelled of ash. She swallowed the burning lump in her throat.

Past the Horning house, she stared at the monstrosity the Manns had built. Massive in size, it loomed over the other houses on the street. Lillian frowned. How many times had she tried to argue against such a monstrosity? Modernize, she'd agreed. Enlarge, she'd said. But no one had listened.

"We need a vacation home for our children and grandchildren," Regina Mann had said, no apology in her voice. "Seven bedrooms, minimum. It's so much better if everyone has their own space, don't you think?"

Regina had torn down the old house with its tin roof and charming porch and built—well, Lillian didn't really know what it was. The outside was pink, the color of that horrible medicine. It had king-sized double doors, Mediterranean arches, and dozens and dozens of lights. They came on like clockwork every night, the glare blinding. She'd often thought it was a wonder they couldn't see that house lit up clear to Charleston. The lines between her brows deepened. Except for last night. While the fire had raged at the Horning house, the Mann mansion had sat dark, like an ominous shadow against the night sky.

"Miss Parker?" said Greg.

"I'm sorry. Were you saying something?"

"I was asking if you've spoken with Trudy since the fire."

"Oh, no, I haven't." Lillian had tried, phoning both Trudy's home and cell numbers but getting only voice mail. "I don't know what to say. Her husband was let go from his job last year, her son broke his leg in a car accident, and now this," she said, lifting her palms. "That house meant everything to her. She might be the only other person on this island who loves this place as much as I do."

He was quiet a moment. "You told one of my men that the fire wasn't an accident."

She sat up straighter. Now they were getting to it. Good. "It wasn't. But you already knew that, didn't you?"

He ran a hand over his head and brushed back his thinning hair. "We don't get many fires like this. Whole place burned to the ground. Only other one I can think of is the one out at the old Crosby place."

She remembered. The Crosby fire had been a doozy, the talk of the town for weeks. Some said Skeet had it coming, but Lillian had never been one to spread gossip. Smokin' Skeet they'd called him, even before the fire. Every day except Sunday, he'd park himself on the bench outside the grocery, a cigarette dangling from his mouth, a brown paper bag in his hand. Most days, he'd nod off in the heat, waking only long enough to take another drink and smoke another pack of Luckys. She'd always thought it was a wonder he hadn't burned down the whole town and not just the pile of wood he called a house. He'd moved off the island after that. Good riddance was all she'd had to say. "Skeet Crosby was an idiot, but he didn't mean to burn down his own house."

"No, I don't suppose he did."

"This one wasn't an accident," she said again.

"I'm interested to hear why you would say that, Miss Parker."

"Because I know who set it." His gaze met hers. "Regina Mann. Do you know Regina?"

"We've met."

She pointed out the window. "Then you also know that horrific thing she calls my house. Regina Mann wants every house on this street, you know. She plans to turn them all into little versions of her house for all her guests. Can you imagine? She probably wants to rename the street Mann Road. She might even get away with it." Her nose wrinkled as she spoke. "The Thurmans sold last month. I did everything I could to talk them out of it, but they said they were planning to move anyway. Going to live with their daughter down in Orlando."

"She wants to buy all the houses on the street?"

"Isn't that what I just said?"

His face flushed pink. "Has she offered to buy your house?"

"More times than I can count." Lillian wagged one finger. "I told her I wouldn't sell to her if I was taking my last breath. She'd do anything to get her hands on every house on this block. Anything." Lillian's voice shook. Regina wasn't above strong-arm tactics and a fire was right up her alley. "That includes the Horning house."

"You don't like Regina Mann."

"The feeling is mutual. I promise you that."

"Any reason other than that she wants to buy your house?"

"No one around here with an ounce of sense likes that woman." Lillian looked him in the eye. "She's not an islander, Greg, and you know it. She doesn't belong here."

He held her gaze a moment, and then he shook his head. "Who belongs here and who doesn't isn't our decision."

Lillian opened her mouth to argue, saw the look on his face— as though he'd eaten something sour or rancid—and thought better of it.

"Look, I've spoken to most of the owners on this street, including the Manns, to let them know about the fire. Mrs. Mann is in New York and has been for the past week. She didn't set that fire."

Lillian shrugged. "Then she hired someone to do it for her."

"Why would she do that?"

"To force Trudy to sell."

"Miss Parker, I know you don't want to hear this, but Mrs. Mann seemed quite upset about the fire. I believe her when—"

"Of course, you believe her. Regina Mann could skin a coon without it even knowing. I'm telling you, that woman cannot be trusted. After this block, it will be the whole neighborhood, then the whole island." Lillian shuddered. "I won't let that happen. I won't."

He leaned forward, the space between them shrinking. "Would it surprise you to know that Mrs. Mann expected you to accuse her?"

"Nothing that woman says or does surprises me."

"You can't blame Mrs. Mann for everything. You've sent countless letters to the editor about her."

"Your wife tell you that, Greggie?" Lillian didn't wait for an answer. "Shouldn't she be out reporting instead of reading my letters?"

"I didn't say she read them," he said.

"Well, I sure wish someone would. Not one of them has been printed. Carl Jenkins is a weak excuse for an editor if ever there was one."

He let out a long breath, plucked at the fabric of his pants. "It's not just the letters. You've phoned the radio, hounded your neighbors." He paused. "You're lucky Mrs. Mann doesn't have you charged with slander."

"She doesn't dare. She wants my house."

He shook his head. "How far are you going to go with this vendetta, Miss Parker?"

The blood rushed to her face. Even if she had sent letters and made calls, so what? She'd done nothing illegal. "You have no right to speak to me that way."

Outside, the wind whipped up and flecks of ash floated past the window and out to the dunes. She squeezed her eyes shut, blinking back the tears. She couldn't smell the ocean air or the sweet summer breeze, only the acrid odor of charred timber and melted plastic. It wasn't right. She couldn't let Regina get away with it. She couldn't let Regina win.

When he spoke again, there was sadness in his voice. "The island has changed, Miss Parker. It doesn't matter whether we want it to or not. Nature does her thing and we do ours. Families come and go; new houses are built. Old houses are bought and sold. There are new businesses to replace the old ones. That's just the way it is. We can't stop change any more than we can stop time." He hesitated. "You can't stop it."

Lillian stiffened. He sounded like Regina.

Greg cleared his throat and she raised her eyes to his. The pain in her back throbbed and she winced. The doctors had said the tumor was inoperable, terminal. They'd offered chemotherapy, of course, but she'd declined. Why did she need it at her age? Regina had been right though. She wouldn't live forever. She wouldn't live out the year.

Out loud, she said, "I'm an old woman, Greg. Set in my ways. Isn't that what they say? When you get to be a certain age, you just get set in your ways."

"Maybe, but you can't stop change. It happens whether you want it to or not." He paused. "When was the last time you saw Trudy Trimble?"

Lillian sat back, dizzy with the change in subject, dizzy with the pain that never stopped. "Friday, I guess. I took her some zucchini bread when she got in for the weekend. It's her favorite. I've been making it for her since she was a girl."

"Did you talk about Regina Mann?"

Lillian frowned again. They'd talked about Regina several times before, but not that night. "No. It was late by the time she got in. After ten already."

"What did you talk about?"

Lillian's shoulders drooped. They hadn't talked about anything. Trudy hadn't invited her in, claiming she was tired. "Nothing."

"You're sure?"

"Of course, I'm sure," she snapped. "I gave her the bread, and I went home. When I woke up the next morning, she'd slipped a note under my door saying she'd had to go back home."

He rose, moving to the large window that faced the ocean. The waves crashed and washed over the sand, stopping only feet from the tall grasses that protected the dunes. Behind the dunes, the houses hugged the narrow strip of beach.

"It's high tide," he said.

Gray clouds hung low over the horizon. An afternoon storm would blow in and out again, leaving a stretch of rainbow over the sea. Like the dramatic tides, the storms were a way of life. Lillian wouldn't have had it any other way. Looking past him, she could see the orange marker protruding from the tallest dune, marking a nest of sea turtles. They needed protecting now, the baby turtles. That's all she was trying to do with the letters and the phone calls. Protect this way of life she'd grown to love. Protect her home. Protect Trudy.

Greg looked over his shoulder. "Did you know that the Manns have a security system?"

She exhaled, wincing. "Of course, they do. They have everything."

"Their security system includes several cameras. One of them faces the Horning house." He turned, searching her face, scrutinizing her as if he didn't know her. His voice was flat, emotionless. "The footage we've been able to access gives us a pretty good idea of when the fire was started. And how."

Lillian's fingernails dug into the skin of her palms and her heart raced. This was it. "Did you see who set the fire?"

Ignoring the question, he said, "The camera showed the flames starting in two places from inside the house."

"Two?"

"The kitchen on the western end, closest to the Manns, and another room on the eastern end, on your side. Spread so fast, the fire destroyed the house before we could get here."

"Well," she said, "there you have it. Regina is nothing if not smart."

"Regina Mann was in New York, Miss Parker. I told you that."

"Mr. Mann then, or someone who works for them."

"No." Greg averted his eyes, shifted his weight from one foot to the other. "Do you have a gas can, Miss Parker?" Lillian's heart thudded in her ears and cold fingers crawled up her spine. This wasn't how it was supposed to go. "I can ask for a search warrant if I need to."

Anger flared again. "You will do no such thing, young man." She touched a hand to her head, smoothing her already combed hair. "Of course, I have a gas can. The boy who mows my front yard on Saturdays uses it to fill the mower."

"The tape showed someone leaving the Horning house." He held up his hand. "No, the face isn't visible. Whoever went in and out of that house knew to hide their face. But there are some things that help identify the, uh, arsonist."

Seconds ticked by. "Well, don't keep me in suspense. Spit it out."

He shoved his large hands deep into his pockets. "This person was small, below average height, like you." Her heart beat faster with each word. "The person moved very slowly, in the direction of your house, using a cane with one hand and carrying a gas can in the other. A bright yellow gas can with something painted on it."

Lillian's breath caught in her throat. Trudy's children had decorated her gas can, given it to her for her birthday last year along with painted flowerpots and a new mailbox.

"What color is your gas can, Miss Parker?"

"Yellow is a common color."

He took a step forward. The sky behind him darkened. "Where is the gas can now?"

She pressed her lips together.

"Mrs. Mann didn't set that fire, Miss Parker. This vendetta you've waged against Mrs. Mann has worried a lot of people. According to the Thurmans, you called their children and their neighbors after they sold to Mrs. Mann. You threatened them. You've become unreasonable. It's got to end now."

"I never threatened anyone. They're only saying that because they sold out."

"They moved. It's not a crime."

She heard the steady plunk of rain against the large window.

"Mrs. Mann said Trudy agreed to sell her house last week, last Friday, in fact." The color drained from Lillian's face. "She told you Friday, didn't she? Is that when you found out? When you took her the bread? Did you get angry? Is that why she left in such a hurry?"

Every part of Lillian's body went numb. Her legs. Her arms. Her mind. She saw his lips move but heard nothing.

"Were you angry with her, Miss Parker? Angry that she would sell and worse, to the one person you hated most, Regina Mann?" He paused to take a breath. Lightning cracked in the distance and thunder echoed over the water. Rain pounded against the roof and windows. "You knew her husband was out of work, that they needed money. She was depressed. Did you know that? Did you know she was seeing a doctor?"

Lillian's head came up. "Who told you Trudy was depressed?"

"Her husband. Their marriage is breaking up. He's very concerned."

Lillian snorted. Trudy's husband had the sensitivity of a snake. If he thought she was depressed, it could only be because she wanted him to think that. Trudy had hired a detective and a lawyer, not a doctor. "What did Mrs. Mann tell you about buying the Horning house?"

"Why does it matter now?" Greg asked.

She almost laughed at the blank look on his face. "Indulge me."

Greg hesitated, and then shrugged. "She only said they came to a verbal agreement on Friday. Trudy would sell her house to Mrs. Mann at the end of the month."

"A verbal agreement."

"The papers were supposed to be signed tomorrow."

"And now?"

"I don't know. Mrs. Mann seemed desperate to reach Mrs. Trimble."

"I bet she did." Lillian sat back again, a slow smile spreading across her lined face.

What a brilliant young woman Trudy was. How long had she been planning the fire? Lillian knew she'd been packing up pictures and mementos for weeks. "I need these at home with me," she'd said. "With everything going on, they give me comfort." Trudy had known about the Mann's camera, even commenting on it once. "It gives me the creeps, you know, having this thing watching our every move. I look away every time I go in and out the door." The cane was the perfect touch.

And Regina Mann had handed Trudy the perfect opportunity. By overpaying for every property on the street, she'd doubled the value of the remaining houses. Arson might not pay when you burned your own house down, but it did when someone else started the fire—someone on video with a yellow gas can and a cane. Trudy would collect and keep her land. The house might be lost, but Lillian wasn't worried.

"I found the old house plans," Trudy had told her not long ago. "The ones my great-grandfather used. If anything ever happens to this house, I'll rebuild it exactly the same." She'd squeezed Lillian's hand. "I promise you that."

"Nothing's going to happen to it," Lillian had said.

"I know," Trudy had smiled, "but just in case."

"Where is the gas can, Miss Parker?" Greg asked.

Lillian looked back at him. When had Trudy borrowed the yellow gas can? Last week? The week before? It didn't matter. "I don't remember," she said. "It's kind of a blur."

"Is it empty?"

Lillian felt sure it was but said nothing. Outside, the rain had stopped. The sky was turning blue, the kind of blue that made Lillian want to drink it in, to fill her soul with its light and purity. Just for a moment, the pain fell away.

"I'm really sorry, Miss Parker. I'm going to have to put this in my report." He lowered his voice. "I don't know what will happen after that."

She nodded. She knew.

There would be a scandal. They'd call her something like Crazy Old Miss Parker or something worse. That's the way these things worked. But she was old and sick, and she didn't mind. Lillian would stay in her house, and she'd die long before the case ever got to trial. And after she was gone, Trudy would get the house, thanks to Regina. It was her parting comment that had prompted Lillian to update her will, making Trudy her beneficiary. It was a fitting bequest, she thought. The Horning house and the Parker house. They were two of a kind after all. Regina might get most of the houses, but she'd never get those.

Lillian looked back at Greg, her eyes bright. "You do what you have to do."

WHO KILLED BILLY JOE?

GENILEE SWOPE PARENTE

Chief of Police Clareese Guidry's head was down in concentration and her mind was on the homicide scene she'd just left. She was headed to Verna's Cajun Café, the local family diner and central hub of information in the small Louisiana town of New Iberia.

The murder victim was Billy Joe Randolph, a thirty-six-year-old male. Billy Joe had been a popular figure in New Iberia, coach of the local Little League, active in church and the town's public information officer. He'd come to town a little more than a year ago and quickly became an important part of the community. The local newspaper ran a feature just last week about his campaign to build a badly needed children's medical clinic. Many people talked about him as if he were a saint.

Yet someone had whacked Billy Joe with a baseball bat, cut him with a sharp tool, and shot him in his office. Clareese pictured Billy Joe's body lying where a janitor had found him this morning, on his back, his eyes open and staring at the ceiling. She would have described the look on his face as shock. How could someone determined to savagely murder him have surprised him?

The whole situation didn't make much sense. Other than a few stray pieces of paper on the floor, there were no signs of a struggle in the office. Nothing was reported stolen. Crime scene processors had dusted for prints and found many, but Billy Joe had hundreds of visitors to his office at City Hall.

The prints on the bat lying next to his body had yielded no match in the criminal database. The rifle on the floor had only Billy Joe's prints—it was his own 22-caliber hunting rifle. They'd found no bloody instrument in the office that could explain the gashes near the bullet hole.

Billy Joe's body was positioned next to a small table holding building plans for the new clinic. Claresse surmised he had been going over the specs when someone attacked him. He fell or was knocked to the floor and landed face up with one arm flung across his chest. He had no defensive wounds on his hands.

Claresse couldn't tell if the blow to his head or bullet wound to his chest was the cause of death. The gashes were on his leg and not very deep so they weren't the cause. She hoped the coroner's report would shed some light on the cause of death and maybe confirm her theory that this crime was unplanned and fueled by passion.

The preliminary autopsy report was due in shortly—the coroner and the body had left the office for the county morgue an hour ago.

It was just after lunch, but Verna's was sure to be full and buzzing with the terrible news. She wanted to catch that buzz and sniff out a few leads. Besides, she badly needed a decent cup of coffee before heading back to her office.

As Clareese expected, the diner was packed. She ordered a large, no-sugar, touch-of-cream and started listening to the talk, asking a few pointed questions to start conversations.

"No, I don't know of anyone who might have wanted to hurt him or anyone who was upset with the man," said Roberto Herbert, the local barber. Billy Joe frequented that shop at least once a week for a personal shave. "I mean, he even got along with Tommy Lee. And you know there ain't many people who Tommy even talks to."

True, thought Clareese. Tommy Lee Bowens, who swept hair at the shop for a few dollars a day, rarely talked to anyone. He was a mentally challenged seventeen-year-old whose frequent bruises and trips to the emergency room led Clareese to suspect the boy's alcoholic father took out his anger on his son.

She turned to listen as Beatrice Jardin piped up. "Billy broke off with Diane a couple of weeks ago you know," she said. "I don't think he was dating anyone else, though I heard Betty Jones has a huge crush on him." Her eyes had that unnatural gleam of someone who wanted to share gossip and knew she shouldn't. The look appeared frequently on her face since Beatrice was the owner of Bea-YOU-tiful, a nail salon that served as another local gathering spot. Only Herbert's Cut 'N Shave and Verna's Cajun Café got better buzz.

The next speaker was the shy, well-liked Alana LeBlanc, the town librarian. "I read in Crime Weekly that a quarter of all murders are committed by family members," she said. "But that can't be the case with Billy Joe. He told me once he isn't close to any family, and they are all somewhere out west." Clareese made a note to check that out.

New Iberia's Mayor Richard Boudreaux Johnson coughed and straightened his tie as if about to make a speech, a gesture he probably used several times a day. All eyes turned to the official.

"It's Billy Joe, *people*," he said. "You know he only had the interests of this town in mind." Clareese knew, however, that the mayor tended to weigh any soul's worth on what resources the person contributed to the community—the idea for the children's clinic gave Billy Joe a huge star in the mayor's eyes.

Clareese took a few more notes as people talked, but she already knew much of what they were sharing. The victim was a bachelor who spent a lot of time at work, dated Diane and a couple of local women before her, had an outgoing personality, lived in Mrs. Gordon's boarding house, and was adored by the kids he coached. He'd started the drive to raise funds for the clinic about nine months ago, a project that had caught fire in town in recent weeks.

The chief closed her notebook and was about to head out the door when a comment from Ralph Schmidt sitting at the counter stopped her.

"What happens now with the money Billy Joe collected for the clinic? Guess we'll have to find someone else to take that over."

Everyone looked around at everyone else. No one seemed to know exactly how it was handled—only that they'd all helped in the fundraising efforts.

"Last Monday at the town meeting, Billy Joe reported the townspeople had saved $250,000 already," said Selma Mae Jenkins, the clerk responsible for taking notes at the council meetings. Her voice grew wistful. "Everyone was so proud of him. That's a lot to raise in just a few months."

"Maybe we should look into how we get that money into an official fundraising account," said George Pickney, the mechanic who ran Pickney's Garage and an elder at First Baptist, the church where many of the fundraisers had been held. "I don't suppose he ever thought about what would happen if he up and died on us."

Selma slugged George on the arm. "How can you say such things at a time like this!" George rubbed his arm and looked sheepish.

Well, I guess the money wasn't in a church fund, Clareese thought. Could it be a motive for murder? Was someone trying to get their hands on what had been raised?

Clareese turned to Jim Burke, president of the New Iberia Community Bank, who was sitting at the counter sipping coffee.

"How about it, Jim? Did Joe have a special fund set up for the clinic?" she asked.

Jim's eyes narrowed and focused on his coffee cup.

"I wouldn't know. His money was not in *our* bank."

Okay, Clareese thought, *I guess that's a sore spot for Jim.* But she understood. Most businesses in New Iberia chose to support the only remaining community bank in town. Maybe since Billy Joe wasn't originally from the area, he had an account with one of the nationals. Surely he hadn't kept it all in cash or checks in his office.

She made a note to trace the funds, and then headed out of the diner, deciding to visit Diane Beacon, his most recent girlfriend, on her way back to Town Hall.

Clareese and Diane had been in the same class at New Iberia High School and had coffee occasionally. Diane had gone away to college and returned a teacher at the school; Clareese had moved back to their hometown only recently after a stressful few years of city work.

The last time Clareese saw Diane, she'd been hanging on Billy Joe's arm at one of the clinic fundraisers. Clareese remembered feeling mildly surprised. While Diane's lustrous black locks and curvy body assured she always had admirers, her whip-smart tongue often stopped men in their tracks. She hadn't had many serious beaux.

Billy Joe's charm must have been able to cut through Diane's shell, Clareese thought as she sat across from her classmate.

"He really was a lot of fun," Diane said, taking a sip from her sweating glass. "A breath of fresh air after a day spent trying to teach history to teens who don't care. Billy and I had a good time together."

She smiled through hazel eyes glistening with tears. "I can't believe he's gone like that—murdered in his office! What happened? Who would have done this?"

"We don't know yet. But I'll find out," Clareese promised. "I'm starting with his background and the last few weeks of his life. I know you two were an item for a while. What can you tell me about his background or his family or what was happening with him? Did he have any enemies?"

Diane's finger traced the rim of her glass. "I can't think of anyone who didn't like Billy Joe. As far as his background, I don't have much to contribute. He was a good talker and an even better listener. But he didn't tend to talk about himself much."

"Why did you break up?" Clareese asked.

Diane set the glass on the coffee table and sat back, rubbing her forehead with one hand as if putting her thoughts together.

"You know, I'm not quite sure. When we first started going out, what… like three months or so ago, I was a little smitten. He knew a little bit about a lot of things, and he certainly was attentive—always asking about school and my day and this town—what it was like growing up here, what the people were like. But I couldn't get him to go very deep into who he was. I'm not exactly sure why it all fizzled before it ever got very far."

"Were you upset or was he angry at the break-up?" Clareese asked.

"Not at all. If anything, I was upset with myself. He was a pretty great guy who was doing all this good for the community, and he was so well liked. But I don't know, it just wasn't *there* for me."

On the way back to her car, Clareese got a call from the coroner's office. Dr. Samuel Jenkins's report managed to throw a wrench into the already complicated crime.

"How can that *be*?"

"I don't know the hows, Clareese, just the whats. I'm just telling you—the blows to the head and the twenty-two caliber slug I took out of his leg did not kill this man. He also didn't bleed out, but his lungs were full of fluid."

"The cause of death was *drowning*?"

"No, that's not what I'm saying," Sam said. "His lungs were filled because he had pulmonary edema, which causes excess fluid in the lungs. It's something a lot of people with bad tickers fight. I could see when I pulled out his heart that the organ was in pretty bad shape, but I don't think he knew it. He came to see me several times for colds and other minor things, but he never mentioned any heart difficulties. If he knew, he didn't tell me."

"So you think his heart just gave out on him from the shock?" Clareese said.

"Well," Sam said. "I suppose the blows, bullets and knife wounds could have triggered a reaction. But if I had to guess, and this really is speculation until we get further lab results, I'd say he was poisoned with something that caused heart failure. I found excess saliva as if he'd foamed at the mouth. I sent blood work off to the lab."

Wow, Clareese thought. Someone really wanted this man dead.

"Thanks, Sam."

Clareese hung up and decided to make a quick stop at the boarding house where Billy Joe had lived, which was also on the way back to Town Hall. She wanted to make sure the owner Thera Gordon didn't move anything in the victim's room.

Although Billy Joe had been in New Iberia for more than a year, he had never moved out of his original room. Clareese wondered why someone who made a decent salary hadn't gotten his own place, though Thera's renowned cooking and sweet disposition had kept more than one boarder from leaving.

When Clareese knocked on the front door of the boarding house, a sobbing Thera greeted her.

"I can't believe he's gone," Thera said into her wad of tissues. "He was such a good boarder. He helped me around the house whenever I needed it. Never drank or smoked. Always paid his rent on time, the first of every month."

"Did Billy Joe pay his rent by check?" Clareese asked.

"Yes, of course. He was never more than a day late and his checks never bounced."

"Can I see his room?"

"Of course."

When Thera took Clareese to Billy Joe's room, she was surprised to discover how barren it was, even for a bachelor. A few of Billy Joe's clothes hung in the closet and one dresser drawer contained his undergarments and socks. But there were no personal mementos or pictures of people.

Clareese slapped on some gloves and did a quick search. The dresser and desk revealed nothing but a few receipts for coffee at Verna's, a dry cleaner's receipt from the local Sun Dry and quite a few receipts for restaurants and bars from the big city. He must have been a frequent visitor to New Orleans, which was surprising given that it was over two hours away.

At the door, Clareese turned back to the heartbroken Thera. "I don't suppose you have a copy of an old check? I didn't find a checkbook or financial statement of any kind in his room."

"Oh my. I guess I do. Today is the second. I haven't yet made it to the bank." She turned, hurried to her office and returned with a check.

"First Bank of New Orleans," Clareese said.

Another connection to the city.

"Do you know if Billy Joe moved here from New Orleans?" she asked.

Thera shook her head. "I don't think so. I think he said he was born and raised in California where his family lives. I guess I never really asked."

Clareese tucked the check in her pocket promising Thera she'd return it after making a copy. Clareese needed to search his office again, call the bank and investigate a new name she saw on the check. *William Joseph Randolph.* No one around town had ever called him anything but Billy Joe.

She returned to Billy Joe's office, searched his desk again and found the checkbook in his desk drawer. There was also a statement from the bank showing William Randolph had a savings account of $275,601. If these were the funds for the clinic, Clareese wondered why the man hadn't set up a charitable account to avoid taxes. And if this truly was his own personal savings account, why did he live like a pauper?

As she rummaged through the drawers, she found something she was afraid might be the answer. It was a plane ticket confirmation email printed in William Joseph Randolph's name dated for three days from now. The ticket was for Puerto Vallarta in Mexico. Clareese would have thought it was a planned vacation, except for the fact it was one-way.

Was the man planning to skip town with the clinic money? Had someone found out and killed him in anger?

A call to the bank threw more fuel on the fire. An executive reported that William Randolph had closed his savings account and transferred the funds to a foreign bank.

Clareese now sat at Billy Joe's desk, wondering how she would break it to the town that they'd been duped. The saintly Billy Joe had not been the person everyone thought he was. But who had found out? And why the overkill?

The door creaked open. Tommy Lee stood on the threshold, tears streaming down his face. Clareese got up and went to the teenager, pulling him inside the office, sitting him down on a chair, and then fetching a tissue.

"I'm sorry, Tommy. I know that Billy Joe was a friend and you're sad."

Tommy's head began to shake back and forth, gently at first, then more vigorously. He grabbed his middle and leaned forward in the chair.

Clareese tried to give him a comforting pat, but she wasn't surprised when Tommy Lee shrank away from the touch. She knew he didn't like anyone to get too close physically.

"He... he said he'd teach me. I didn't mean to hurt him," Tommy was hiccupping as he talked, close to hysteria.

Hurt Billy Joe? Oh lord. Had Tommy been the murderer?

Clareese didn't say anything. Silence was a better tool at this point than anything she might say to alarm him. The boy would get out what he came to say if she gave him time.

"He promised me he'd teach me," the boy repeated. "I was just practicing. I tried to save him."

What on earth was the boy talking about?

"Billy Joe promised to teach you what?" Clareese said, careful to keep her tone even.

"I'm tired of being the water boy. I wanted to play. I should have waited."

Ah. Billy Joe must have told Tommy he'd coach him. A picture of the bat formed in her head.

"Coach Randolph was going to teach you to play baseball? Well, that's good, Tommy. I'm sure you'd be great. Waited for what, though?"

"To bat the ball... He said he'd give me lessons, but not until tomorrow. He said he was going hunting today with his friend, but he'd teach me tomorrow. I should have waited."

Clareese pictured the bruising on Billy Joe's head and arm.

"Did you have an accident, Tommy?"

The tears and hiccupping picked up pace.

"I had... I had the bat with me. I just wanted to show him I could do it. I didn't mean to hit him. He fell down there." Tommy pointed to a spot on the floor, a few feet away from where the body was found.

Clareese got a second chair and sat across from the boy, waiting for some of the hysteria to pass. After five minutes and a few more tissues, she asked: "Tell me what happened, Tommy. What happened to the coach?"

"I swung the bat real hard. He fell down and bumped his head on that table. His rifle fell down with him, and I heard a shot."

Tommy looked directly at Clareese for the first time, his tear-filled eyes begging for understanding. "I thought I could save him. I thought I could help."

"What did you do after he fell and the rifle went off, Tommy?"

"I done what they always do on T.V. I got out the knife my grandpa gave me, and I tried to get the bullet out to save him, but I kept dropping it. He started cussing at me something fierce, just like my papa does when he's real mad. I didn't like the shouting, but I didn't talk back. I never do. I just done what I do for Daddy. I got him his brown bottle."

Clareese looked around the office again, trying to spot a brown bottle.

"Where did you get a brown bottle, Tommy? Where is it now?"

"I left it in that bathroom," Tommy pointed to a nearby door.

Clareese knew it led to a small washroom. She got up and walked to the room, where she saw a couple of bottles sitting next to each other on the floor. One of them had a black label and held brown liquid. It easily could have passed for Jack Daniels to someone who couldn't read well and wasn't thinking straight.

She walked back into the office and held it out to Tommy.

"Is this the bottle?" she asked.

Tommy nodded. "I put it to his mouth and he gulped it down, but he spit it out right at me! I put the bottle back where it belonged and got some water from the bathroom instead, but when I came back to him, I got scared. His eyes looked all funny and he was breathing hard and cussin'. I jumped up and ran out of there. I tried to tell my daddy when I got home, but Daddy wouldn't wake up, just like always. And then... and then I just went into my room and hid."

"But you knew you needed to come back today to check on him." Clareese kept her voice gentle and soothing. Tommy looked up at her again, and she could see the raw fear and sorrow in his tear-filled eyes.

"I wanted to make sure he's okay. He ain't okay, is he?"

"No, he's not okay, Tommy," Clareese said. "But I don't think you meant to hurt him. You can come down to my office, and we'll sort it all out."

Clareese gestured toward the door, not surprised when Tommy obeyed and walked past her, shoulders slumped, eyes to the ground. There'd be no need to put this boy in handcuffs.

She picked up the bottle of drain cleaner and followed Tommy out the door.

A JOB TO DIE FOR

DEB ROLFE

I'm a natural born killer at heart and get paid pretty well for it. But if it wasn't for a very rocky start in an advertising agency, my murder M.O. would be much less interesting.

Fifteen years ago I was a recent college graduate with a BFA and ninety thousand words of a mystery novel in my laptop. While my dream was to be a full-time writer, I needed steady income to pay the bills. So I sent out a dozen résumés, confident of quickly snagging a desk job.

Not being snapped up in the first month was disappointing to say the least. I scoured the job listings again and submitted more résumés. Finally, the Schmitt Agency called to schedule an interview for the position of executive assistant. The next day I donned my favorite wrap dress, a splurge for my graduation day, and drove to their offices on the outskirts of Charlottesville.

The receptionist told me to take a seat until Mr. Schmitt was free. Beyond the lobby wall I heard an angry growl berating someone about unacceptable work. Feet stomped away. A door slammed. The receptionist shook her head as she picked up the phone and announced my arrival.

I was directed to Frank Schmitt's office and leaned across the wide desk to shake hands. His palm was clammy and the top of his head sported a blond toupee that didn't match the graying hair around his ears. I was already nervous and watching his eyes drill down the V-neck of my dress didn't help any.

I freed my hand and forced a smile. "I'm Raleigh Myers. I've heard excellent things about your company."

"Unusual name. Why Raw-lee?" he asked, stringing out the syllables.

"My father traveled for work. I have sisters named Savannah and Charlotte. We were always happy Dad's territory didn't include Walla Walla."

Schmitt grunted. "That would be funny if a little kid said it."

Did he insult everyone in interviews? Was this to judge my reaction? I decided to let it pass. He signaled for me to take a seat, looking me over from head to bust line.

"What exactly would be my responsibilities?" I asked.

"Your duties are rather fluid. Are you good at working independently and handling details?"

"Extremely. In college I managed a heavy class load while also volunteering…"

"Fine, fine. But what caught my attention are your special interests." He stabbed one finger at the piece of paper centered on his desk. "Genealogy, gourmet cooking, exotic fish, and bonsai trees."

My heart dropped to my stomach. Most of what I knew about my "special interests" came from Wikipedia.

He pointed to an oak credenza where three dwarf trees sat in shallow dishes. "What do you think?"

"They're very attractive."

"Greenhouse guy said pruning bonsai is an art. Bet you could give me some pointers."

I remembered reading that clipping the wrong leaf could irrevocably ruin the appearance. "I'd have to study them for a while before making any suggestions."

"Ah, so you do have some expertise. Excellent." He continued staring. "Don't have any damn dogs or cats, do you? I'm allergic to pet dander."

"No, sir." The only pet I could afford to feed was a one-eyed beta fish that lived in a recycled pickle jar.

"Good, good. Got any questions?"

I had many. "Will my lack of experience be a problem?"

"Assuming you can already write coherent sentences, you'll pick up the rest as you go. That is, unless you're a complete imbecile."

Writing was my passion. Getting paid to write would be perfect. "And what's the starting salary?"

"How much you want?"

I had researched pay scales for the area. The number I gave him was, I believed, reasonable.

He sneered. "Half that to begin." He looked me over again. "Maybe an occasional bonus so you can buy something decent to wear. Can you start tomorrow?"

I glanced down uncertainly at my dress. The jerk had crossed the line with that remark. I wanted to walk out but I really needed this job. "Sure. What time?"

Instead of answering, he bellowed, "Ruth, get in here."

The staccato tapping of heels on tile preceded the receptionist's appearance in the doorway.

"Make her official," he said. "And cancel Bill's bonus. He hasn't earned it this month."

Ruth touched my shoulder and nodded for me to follow her. We passed the small office next door.

"That's yours," she said and then continued toward the lobby.

I took the chair beside her desk, clutching my purse on my lap. "May I ask why his previous assistant left?"

"A problem with her nerves." Ruth shrugged. "Now, your hours will be eight-thirty to five. Medical benefits come after thirty days. Frank encourages creativity, but he knows what works and what doesn't. I've been here over twenty years and can handle criticism. If you can't, then consider taking a pass on this offer."

My mind was spinning. "I'm ready to do my very best for Frank."

She lowered her voice. "Address him as Mr. Schmitt. People only call him Frank behind his back. Among other things." The corners of her mouthed twitched. "We'll see you tomorrow unless you change your mind."

"I'll be here."

Her phone rang, and she waggled fingers in the air towards me. I'd been dismissed.

That evening I pulled everything out of my closet, wondering what was "decent" enough for an Executive Assistant to wear. Ruth's outfit probably came from one of the downtown boutiques but I'd have to stick to department store sale racks for a while.

I was too excited to sleep well, floating on air to have found the perfect job for my creative mind. I rose early to spend extra time on my hair and makeup. Worried about traffic, I left too soon and had to wait in my car until Ruth arrived to unlock the door.

"Good morning," she said. "So you decided to give us a try after all." The phone started ringing and Ruth pointed toward the hallway. "Go on back. I'll be with you shortly." Before I could respond, she picked up the phone.

My office seemed darker than I remembered, with no window and only an overhead fluorescent light that flickered. I was glad I hadn't thrown out my desk lamp from college. The drawers revealed basic office supplies and a sticky note reading *$cHmitt@genCy*.

Ruth strolled in. "Frank is out this morning. I see you found the computer password. Not very creative for a business like this, is it?"

"What exactly does the Schmitt Agency do?"

"Seriously? You didn't ask before?" She plopped onto the other chair, which wobbled a bit. "We're creative marketing consultants. We develop comprehensive advertising campaigns, mostly for wineries and breweries."

I grinned. "And there's no shortage of those around here."

"Exactly, but we handle other clients, too. Frank comes up with the overall concept and our people take it from there. When we're swamped or understaffed like now, we sometimes subcontract out the detailed design work to independent graphics studios in the area.

"He's a wizard at this stuff and the rest of us do our best to keep up. Penny's our local service rep but she called in sick today. I suspect she's really interviewing for another job. Bill's our in-house artist and project designer. Mike writes copy and musical jingles. And I handle all the front office duties."

I heard her phone ringing in the distance. She leaned over, pushed a flashing red button on my desk phone and answered the call. When she hung up, I got a quick lesson in transferring calls and sending them to voice mail. Then she gave me a tour to point out the restroom, lunchroom, and other offices.

She introduced me to Bill, hunched over a light table in an incredibly cluttered workspace. He looked me up and down before grunting, "Welcome to Hades."

"Be nice now," Ruth said.

"She looks too perky. That'll drive Frank crazy. Crazier." He laughed and returned to his work.

Ruth sighed and led me back down the hall. "Don't mind him. He's been here five years and thinks that gives him the right to be rude." We entered Mr. Schmitt's executive suite. "Over there's a private bathroom. If he yells about needing extra towels, they're in the credenza."

I was getting the impression Mr. Schmitt yelled a lot. The phone rang again and she answered it from his desk. It appeared the conversation might be an extended one, so I returned to my office and spent the rest of the morning poking around in the computer programs. It was a relief to see familiar icons on the screen. If nothing else, I'd be able to type up any reports or correspondence Mr. Schmitt needed.

He called around two. "Raw-lee, run out and pick up my dry cleaning. Ruth has the ticket. See you tomorrow."

I grabbed my purse and went to the front office. "I'm supposed to go to the cleaners."

Ruth frowned. "But he said… oh, never mind." She opened her top drawer and handed over a claim ticket. "Champion Cleaners, back towards town, on the right. Sign has blue neon soap bubbles, Frank's design. Charge it to his account."

I followed her directions and returned within half an hour. Ruth glanced up from her monitor.

"That was quick. Hang those on the hook behind his office door."

She turned back to her computer, sending the message that even if I wasn't busy, she had plenty of things to do. I left her alone for the rest of the day while I looked up everything I could find on bonsai trees. By the time I went home, I had a throbbing headache from the constantly blinking ceiling light.

The next morning, I was bent over, plugging in my desk lamp, when I heard my boss shout.

"Dammit to hell. Raw-lee, get in here," Mr. Schmitt shouted.

I grabbed a note pad and pen and dashed next door. "Yes, sir?"

He was snatching papers away from a puddle of coffee spreading across his desk. "Don't just stand there. Do something."

I yanked open the credenza door and grabbed a hand towel to soak up the spill, then hung the stained towel in the bathroom. The whole time Frank expounded on details of the new contract he'd finalized with a Staunton craft brewery.

"So let's see what your salary is buying me. Come up with a couple of ideas by tomorrow. Slogans, brochures, special events." He glared at me and snarled, "Well, what are you waiting for? Go. Time is money."

I returned to my office, excited about brainstorming an entire marketing campaign. My mind raced, and I filled pages with notes and sketches. At last I could put my creativity to good use.

The next morning I was ready to unveil three promotions, certain any one of them would be acceptable.

After the first presentation, he said, "That's atrocious. Next."

I had mentally tried to prepare for rejection, but it still stung. I forced myself to shake it off and dove into the second proposal.

"Absolutely not," he said. No explanation, no suggestions, nothing.

By then my linen sheath was limp with perspiration. I blew a puff of air up towards a droopy curl. My third presentation was far less enthusiastic, and I dreaded hearing his verdict.

He frowned. "What else have you got?"

"Nothing else, sir."

"All those years of college and that's the best you can do? I should fire you, but I'll give you another shot. Come up with something better by tomorrow. Now get all this crap out of here."

I juggled my posters, flip chart, and note cards through the doorway but dropped half in the hall when I bumped into someone.

"Here, let me help you with those," he said.

I stumbled into my office and deposited my "crap" on the desk. The man followed and added the rest to the pile.

"I'm Mike Garrett." His mouth curved up into a crooked grin. "Having fun yet?"

"Raleigh Myers. I'm not sure fun's the right word."

He laughed. "You'll get used to it. Or not. Can't believe I've lasted almost a year. I just stopped by to update my account files, and then I'm out of here. Good luck." That was the last time I saw him. Mike failed to mention he was resigning.

I struggled for new ideas for the brewery promotion and had only one more done by end of day. I carried my materials home that evening and had a major breakthrough. I fleshed out an alternate campaign by midnight and slept well, believing I'd come up with winners for tomorrow's presentation.

Mr. Schmitt didn't agree. He quickly shot down both proposals. "I'm very disappointed. Thought a fancy college graduate would be full of ideas to promote a brewery."

My shoulders slumped. "I'm sorry, sir. But I've never done anything like this before."

"Grow up, Raw-lee. This is the real world. Did making excuses get your professors to raise your grades? I seriously doubt it." He laughed. "Thank God I wasn't relying on you for this new account. This was just a test. I've already come up with the perfect theme and have an outside designer fleshing it out. Sit in on our meeting next week. Might learn something."

I was speechless. I'd worked my butt off on my own time for nothing. And that moment was when I decided Schmitt must become a victim in my next novel. Someone who deserved to die, but not by any ordinary means. My short time in his presence confirmed his worthiness of only the most unusual departure for the great beyond.

Perusing the Internet over the weekend, I discovered African poison darts. An online dealer offered a hand-carved blowgun and pointy-tipped projectiles. Might take some practice with the thoughtfully provided dummy darts before my killer got the hang of it, but a well-placed shot would dispatch the victim before he ever knew what hit him.

Monday began badly and went downhill. Ruth was right about Penny, who emailed in her resignation. Frank was furious over the "lack of loyalty" from Penny and Mike and took it out on everyone who crossed his path. The contract designer on the brewery campaign walked out in the middle of his presentation after Frank questioned his intelligence. I silently applauded his audacity, then slipped back to my office, hoping to lie low for the rest of the day.

"Raw-lee, get in here."

I dragged myself to face him.

"Here, I got these for you." He handed me small silvery clippers. "Specially designed for bonsai trees. Let me know when you're ready to try them out."

I examined the curved blades, wondering if they could "accidentally" whack off a man's fingertips and whether he'd bleed to death before the EMT's arrived. Or maybe he would contract an incurable exotic disease from the bonsai sap. This would require more research.

Mr. Schmitt interrupted my thoughts, stirring one hand in a circle. "Turn around."

I did a slow pirouette, proud of the tailored designer shirtdress picked up in a consignment shop.

He frowned. "Wear something more professional tomorrow. We'll be calling on local clients. Ruth will give you the list. Familiarize yourself with their current campaigns."

I tried my best, took copious notes but didn't understand much of what I read. That night I pressed my navy suit and white blouse, praying they'd be professional enough for Mr. Schmitt.

He groaned when he saw me. "You look like a funeral director. Undo a few buttons on that blouse and loosen up a little."

I accompanied him around town where I was introduced as Penny's temporary replacement. Mr. Schmitt did all the talking while I played wallflower, embarrassed to be excluded from conversations as if this was Take Your Daughter to Work Day.

On the way back to the office, he chewed me out. "If you're gonna be in sales, you gotta learn to speak up."

But I didn't want to be in sales. I imagined unleashing poisonous Australian funnel-web spiders and watching them crawl up inside his pants legs. Or maybe a small venomous coral snake, native to Virginia but seldom seen. Either would do the trick if I could manage not to get bitten too.

Near day's end I passed Bill's office, glanced in, and did a double take. The room was tidy, a single sheet of paper on his desk. I tiptoed in to read it: "I hereby tender my resignation effective immediately. William Mercer."

I eased out and went home for the day, leaving that particular bombshell to be discovered by someone else.

Violent nightmares riddled my sleep, visions of a body strapped to a light table while swinging sheets of crisp paper sliced neatly into flesh. I awoke with premonitions of personal distress.

Ruth confirmed my suspicions as soon as I arrived. "Frank's on the warpath. Bill left without giving notice."

Almost immediately I heard, "Raw-lee, is that you?"

"Yes, Mr. Schmitt, coming."

"Thank God you've got more scruples than the others. Good riddance, I say. Now I've got a plan to give us a shot in the arm. Gonna send a mail blast to the entire client list. Want you to write a letter that will grab 'em by the balls. Get them excited about all the new income we'll help generate. Come up with something to have our phone ringing off the hook, and do it before lunch."

Okay, this was right up my alley. I'd aced all my writing classes and could surely create the perfect letter. I giggled as my fingers danced across the keyboard.

Mr. Schmitt cursed after my first draft. "Makes us sound desperate. Try again."

And after the second one, "For God's sake, we want them begging us, not the other way around."

He tore up my third letter and slammed his fist on the desk. "I'll write the damn thing myself. Get out of my sight."

I spent the afternoon designing a ceiling-mounted guillotine positioned in Frank's shower, thoughtfully placed to take advantage of the built-in floor drain. I also researched paraquat, wondering if sprinkling the toxic liquid onto towels could transfer a lethal dose to wet skin. Everyone knows how dangerous the bathroom can be.

The next morning, I found Mr. Schmitt's client letter on my desk. It was virtually the same as the first one I'd written the day before. My heartbeat thumped in my ears as I read entire plagiarized sentences. He also left a note ordering me to personalize the salutations by doing a mail merge and to use his signature stamp. The message ended: "AND DON'T SCREW THIS UP."

I immediately envisioned an oversized torture device similar to a wine press. Giant screws would steadily turn to compress two metal plates, squeezing the breath out of the evil villain strapped inside.

Ruth helped me set up the mail merge with the client list. She sounded as relieved as I felt when she commented that Mr. Schmitt was out all day playing golf with clients. By early afternoon, almost a hundred letters were ready to mail.

The office was quiet for a change. Ruth and I sat and talked.

"I suspect this job isn't what you wanted," she said, "but I'm proud of you for trying. Frank was blindsided by the other people quitting so close together, and he's worried about the company's survival. I told him this might be a good time to close up shop for good. He's on numerous heart medications, and I wouldn't be surprised if he dropped dead at his desk one day. You should keep your eyes open for other opportunities."

I didn't tell her I already had an interview scheduled after work tomorrow. "Why have you stayed here so long?"

"Because Frank knows nothing about accounting and mostly leaves me alone. When times were tight, I've gone without being paid, but I'll get it all back with interest." She sighed. "To tell you the truth, I'm exhausted. I told Frank I'm taking a few days off, starting tomorrow. But don't worry, everything's caught up. Your check will be on your desk in the morning. And you won't have to do anything extra except answer the phone."

That was good news, as I had no interest in learning bookkeeping. She handed over an office key and gave me the rest of the afternoon off. I left feeling sick to my stomach, realizing now I'd be stuck alone in the office with my sadistic boss.

First thing the next day, I learned I was too dumb to know the right way to apply postage. Frank pointed at the stack of envelopes in the out basket. "Dammit, you should have used stamps. Looks more personal than the postage meter. Take them to the post office anyway. And then come right back."

After mailing the letters, I stopped by the bank to cash my paycheck. It was rejected for insufficient funds. I went straight to Mr. Schmitt when I returned.

"For God's sake, Raw-lee. You must have misunderstood," he said. "I'll call them myself."

I waited while he talked to several people at the bank, including a vice president. His hand turned white gripping the phone. His bushy eyebrows scrunched together and beads of sweat trickled out from under the toupee as he hung up.

"I don't understand. Ruth's been transferring funds to a numbered account in Belize. Practically cleaned us out. Did she say anything to you before she left?"

"Only that she was taking a few days off."

He stared at me, not yelling, not saying anything. Maybe not believing what I said.

"Excuse me, Mr. Schmitt, but about my paycheck. I need rent money."

"Take what you're owed from petty cash. We'll clear all this up when she returns."

The drawers in Ruth's desk were empty except for an unlocked metal box that held only a handful of change. I showed it to Mr. Schmitt.

"No problem," he said. "I'll transfer money from my personal account so you can cash your check tomorrow. We'll get back on track soon. I'm seeing clients the rest of the week. You plan to start calling on more local accounts."

I looked at the worthless check in my hand. I'd probably never get paid for the hours I'd already worked. "Sorry, sir, but I hereby resign."

"Absolutely not. You can't leave until Ruth comes back."

"No. I'm leaving now."

"Then don't expect a glowing reference from me."

"Doesn't matter. I won't put this job on my résumé anyway, Frank." I started to walk away but a strange sound prompted me to look back.

The man clutched both hands to his chest, his mouth forming an "O" like a cartoonish fish gasping for air. His face was as white as his dress shirt; perspiration flowed down both cheeks. I grabbed the desk phone and dialed 9-1-1.

The EMT's hooked him up to an oxygen tank and heart monitor before wheeling him out. I watched them drive away, siren blaring. And then I was alone.

My eyes landed on the trio of bonsai trees. I imagined leaves and branches flying from flashing blades as I took my revenge. But the plants would likely dry up and die soon anyway. I left the clippers on Frank's desk, unused.

I retrieved my purse and desk lamp and left the Schmitt Agency, dropping the key back through the mail slot. I now had enough time before my interview to run home and change into my favorite wrap dress.

I landed the new job with a regional magazine, which provided connections leading to my first published novel and then five sequels. The original uncashed Schmitt Agency check still hangs framed over my writing desk. And though Frank passed away many years ago, I'll continue to acknowledge him in every book for inspiring me to create interesting ways to die.

After all, murder should be memorable.

JUST LIKE JIMINY CRICKET

RONALD STERLING

After my husband passed away from cancer, I saw my sister's family more often. My only daughter lived in Seattle and my only son in New York. My sister, Emily (née O'Farrell), her husband, Peter Coffee, and their four grown kids all lived in and around Richmond, Virginia. They thought I was lonely, and I let them think that because I enjoyed being included in the family get-togethers.

Emily was my only sibling and eight years my senior. Eight years is enough to bypass any of the common rivalries between sisters of contemporary ages. I never knew anything other than kindness from her. She and her husband Peter started dating in high school and married young, about one month after graduating from college in 1974. Emily found employment as a math teacher in a junior high school in Richmond, and Peter began law school. Several years later, an old Richmond law firm hired Peter and they began their family.

My brother-in-law had engaged the Boathouse at Sunday Park, a charming lakeside restaurant in Chesterfield County, for a sixty-fifth birthday luncheon for Emily. Armed with a well-wrapped engraved silver bowl, I drove the twenty-odd miles from Richmond. It was a very enjoyable luncheon and when the time came to sing the birthday song, the entire wait staff joined us, bearing a three-tiered cake with lighted candles and a bunch of colored balloons. While eating the birthday cake and enjoying the rich coffee, my niece Rosemary slid in beside me. Still slim at thirty-four, despite having given birth to three, her dark tresses hung to her shoulders.

"Aunt Ruth, after this big meal, we're just going to have left-overs tonight for dinner, but I would very much like you to join us. I'm worried about something and need your advice. About seven, okay?"

"Fine, I'll be there."

Rosemary was Emily's third child, and when I was twenty-three, I stood as godmother to her.

The Italians and the Irish share Roman Catholicism, but little else. To the Italians, being a godmother is a lifelong commitment often extending sixty or more years. The duties of an Irish godmother are limited to driving the family and the baby to the church, taking them home after the baptism, and not drinking too much at the Christening party which follows. However, Rosemary and I have always been very close from the time she learned to talk, due to her vibrancy and charm.

True to her word, Rosemary, now dressed in blue jeans and a sweatshirt reading *Cloverleaf Middle School*, placed a platter of cold sliced ham, turkey, and cheese on the table along with leftover bowls of baked beans and macaroni salad, jugs of mustard and mayonnaise, and a loaf of rye bread. Her husband, Jack, opened two bottles of Corona beer and handed me one. Her three children were, as usual, animated and talkative. It was, for the second time that day, an enjoyable meal dampened only by the foreknowledge that something was worrying Rosemary.

Dinner completed, Rosemary and I adjourned to the den, leaving Jack and the kids to clear the table and wash the dishes.

"You might have noticed that my gift to Mom today was a set of pewter candlesticks. That was not what I'd planned to give her. You know how Mom and Dad like to travel."

"I do."

"Two months ago, they went down to the Outer Banks for the weekend and left me to check on the house and feed the cat. I used that opportunity to rifle through the family pictures. You probably know that Mom is averse to picture albums. She keeps all the pictures in old shoeboxes, labeled 1970s, 1980s, 1990s, and 2000s. There were also two boxes dedicated to the O'Farrells and the Coffees taken before Mom and Dad were married."

"Yes, I've seen her bring out some of those boxes. Why is that significant?"

"My idea for a gift was to pick out those photographs taken on their various trips over the years. The one that keyed me up on the idea was taken of the two of them on a senior class trip standing in front of the White House."

"I remember that shot. They're both grinning ear to ear."

"Well, anyway," Rosemary continued, "I went through the boxes searching for pictures taken on trips. Those in black and white, I planned to have colorized and have all the pictures reproduced in uniform size before taking them to a framer."

"What stopped you?" I asked.

"When your objective is a certain type of picture, you gather them together, in this case I collected sixteen photos taken over four decades. Individually, the similarities weren't apparent and gathered no attention. But together, the common thread was hard to ignore."

"What similarities?" I asked.

"Take a good look at the first one," Rosemary said. "It was taken in 1970 when they were seniors in high school."

I studied the photo. It showed the smiling young couple standing outside the iron fence that surrounded the White House. Standing by or walking behind them was perhaps a half dozen other people. "Okay. Nothing remarkable."

"I know, but now look at this one. Dad's parents gave them a honeymoon in Jamaica as a wedding present. Here are Mom and Dad having dinner at the Half Moon Hotel in Montego Bay."

They were seated at a table outdoors in a beautiful setting. The dining tables were partially separated by island vegetation on a large flagstone patio. Other couples could be seen in the background at other tables.

"Notice anything yet?" asked Rosemary.

"No, maybe I'm dense. What should I be looking for? Is it that they're both in the picture? Who is taking the picture?"

"No, that's not it," she said quickly. "There's always some passerby who will usually volunteer to take a picture." She reached for the next picture. "Look at this one. Atlantic City, 1978."

This image featured Peter and Emily on the boardwalk in a rickshaw. In the background, the sky was a vivid blue and the ocean calm. And there was the uniformed rickshaw driver also in the frame.

"Wait a minute." I picked up the shot from Montego Bay taken two years before and thousands of miles away. "The guy at the next table next to your Mom and Dad's looks like the rickshaw driver."

"Bingo!" said Rosemary. "Now look at the one at the White House again."

"Oh my God." I keyed in on a guy walking by. The man appeared to be about fifty years old and was in all three pictures taken years apart at different locations. "How can that be?"

"And here's one taken at Marineland in Florida, and there he is again in 1983. And at the Bronx Zoo in 1985. The Golden Gate bridge in 1987." Rosemary was now dealing out the pictures like so many playing cards.

"The Eiffel Tower in 1991. St. Peter's Cathedral in Rome in '94. Yellowstone National Park with the buffaloes in '95. Niagara Falls in '98, Mount Rushmore in '01, and several others, ending up with them standing in front of the Statue of Liberty just last year. And he is in every one of those shots. Sometimes in profile, sometimes looking directly into the camera."

"There is something very wrong. These pictures cover a period of over forty years, and he looks the same. He never ages. This makes no sense," I said.

"I noticed that," Rosemary said. "What do you think it means?"

"I have no idea. Can't explain it. But whatever the explanation is, it doesn't seem to be a danger to your parents or something would have happened long ago. It didn't. Who else have you talked to about this?"

"Just Jack. No one else."

"I understand what you mean about not seeing this when viewing the pictures the way your mother has them assembled."

"What do you think I should do?" Rosemary asked me, somehow expecting that I would give her sound advice.

"I don't know there's anything to do. If there is, I'm baffled," I said. "There may be other pictures with this guy that are not taken in front of landmarks. Understandably overlooked. Although, I don't know what they would prove. They'd just be icing on the cake. Sixteen times pretty well clinches it."

I drove home, racking my brain for some possible explanation. How could some guy follow my sister and her husband around for decades and never age while so doing? In looking at a picture, one never thinks about who took it. A woman co-worker once told me that her grown son commented that she wasn't around much when he was a little boy.

"Where did you get that idea?" she asked.

"Well, you're not in the any of the pictures," he answered.

"I was the one who *took* the pictures," she explained with some passion. It occurred to me that maybe some of the pictures in Emily's boxes were taken by the mysterious passerby.

* * * *

Months passed.

I had signed up for a bus trip to Nashville sponsored by a singles club to which I belonged. The chartered bus left Richmond at six on a Tuesday morning and arrived in Nashville in time for dinner. Most of the club was tired from the long hours on the road, but a few of the heartier members, including me, went downtown to visit the honky tonks. Many country musicians worked these bars without salary but could usually pick up a few hundred in tips.

On Wednesday, the entire group went for a very enjoyable performance at the original Ryman Auditorium, better known as the "Grand Ole Opry." Thursday sent most of the women shopping but I am not a shopper, so I went with a few of the men on a tour of the Hermitage, the home of Andrew Jackson. It was a stately house with columns, located about ten miles east of Nashville.

A tour guide met us at the front door of the house. As we walked down the center hall, the guide commented about the paintings that bedecked both walls. Most were of General Jackson or his wife Rachel, and I gave them a perfunctory glance. All of these pictures were artists' renderings pre-dating photography. One in particular caught my eye, and I walked another five or six paces before it hit me. I stopped dead in my tracks. I returned to the picture that had grabbed my attention and stared at it in disbelief. The legend beneath the portrait read *General John Coffee—Second In Command at the Battle of New Orleans. 1772—1833*. It was the rickshaw driver, the man outside the White House, the tourist in Jamaica. He was all of them. And his name was Coffee. He had to be an ancestor to my brother-in-law, Peter Coffee.

I sent an e-mail to Rosemary: Rosemary—I came across a painting of General John Coffee in the mansion of Andrew Jackson outside of Nashville. The tour guide said if you Google John Coffee, you'll see the painting. I'll be home on Saturday and will talk to you then. Aunt Ruth; sent from my I-phone.

In the morning, I received an email back from Rosemary:

> *Dear Aunt Ruth—I checked out the portrait on Google, and it's the same man, without a doubt. I called my dad, and he said that his Great Aunt Deliverance Coffee (What a name!) wrote a genealogy many years ago, and it shows that General John Coffee was his 4X great-grandfather. Dad has never been interested in the family tree and so never mentioned it to me or my brothers. But you sure hit pay dirt. It makes me wonder if other people have ancestors following them around. See you Saturday. Love, Rosemary*
> *PS*
> *Looks like my dad has his own guardian angel. That's a handy thing for a lawyer to have. It's kind of like Jiminy Cricket watching out for Pinocchio.*

NEVER MARRY A REDHEAD

S.E. WARWICK

Edith compiled a mental list of seasonal chores as she over-looked the garden behind her home near Virginia's Eastern Shore. Her third husband Henry, the love of her life, had chosen the site for its elevation and inland location to withstand hurricanes. Each tree, shrub, and plant had been selected with care. Edith's prized camellia, placed against a brick wall to shelter it from a killing frost, nearly reached the roof. From her favorite chair, she could see its buds swelling in anticipation of spring.

"You're going to love The Beacons, Mother," Gail gushed from the kitchen as she emptied the dishwasher. "It's like a cruise ship on land. They've got apartments with ocean views and lots of bridge partners for you."

"I'll take care of that later, dear," Edith said aloud, annoyed at her daughter-in-law's insistence on "helping." She always put things in the wrong place.

"There, Mother, all set. You need to be careful of that new hip," Gail replied in a tone reserved for cognitively challenged seven-year-olds. "My realtor friend, Susan, says that homes in this area are selling quickly above asking price."

Edith ignored the real estate report. "I'll wear the cranberry jacket. Its slick fabric helps me slide into the car."

Gail frowned. A photo on an end table caught her attention. "Oh, what a cute picture of Frank and Tom when they were little! I don't think I've ever seen it before." She lifted the silver frame for closer inspection.

"I came across it while looking for something else. We don't want to be late for lunch."

Gail was right. The Beacons did have the aura of a resort. Its lobby was bright, welcoming, scented with fresh flowers, and equipped with subtle handrails for those unsteady on their feet. A perky young woman named Lauren greeted Edith and Gail, and then introduced a silver-haired couple named Ruth and Ed as they sat at a table covered with snowy linen. While they ate, Lauren extolled the virtues of life at The Beacons. Their dining companions nodded in mute agreement, reminding Edith of the sports hero bobble-head dolls her sons had collected when they were boys. Looking around the room, Edith noticed that all of the residents wore medallions that she suspected were call buttons, and most sported dreamy expressions. She wondered if they were on antidepressants.

After lunch, Lauren gave them the grand tour of the complex, finishing at a pleasant third-floor apartment with a sliver of ocean view.

"Your favorite chair would be perfect here with the television there," Gail said, gesturing like a windmill. Edith stood mute.

Back in Lauren's office, the sales pitch began in earnest. "That unit has generated a lot of interest. I don't know how long I can hold it without a deposit," the young woman said, sliding a contract and pen toward Edith. "We could have you moved in by the end of the month."

Edith pushed her chair away from the table and stood up. "Thank you so much for your time and the tour. Fetch my jacket, please, Gail." Lauren looked at Gail, who now glared at Edith.

"Mother, wait, we need to talk about this." Gail hurried after her mother-in-law, who was striding toward the door. "I'll call you later," Gail told Lauren over her shoulder.

Edith was furious at her daughter-in-law's latest attempt to remove her from the home she loved. Gail, who had been designated to "take care of mother," finagled the sale of Edith's car after her hip surgery in the hope that the resulting isolation would encourage her to move to a congregate care facility. Her great-granddaughter Phoebe, however, had introduced Edith to Uber. A true "ginger," Phoebe was the only one of Edith's descendants to inherit her bright red hair.

Gail had a conniption the first time she arrived at Edith's home to find the older woman gone, and even more furious when her mother-in-law explained. "You were absolutely right about my giving up the car. These nice Uber chauffeurs pick me up and drop me off at the door of wherever I'm going. For an extra tip, they're happy to carry my things inside. Much nicer than driving myself."

"But that's so expensive," Gail complained.

"So what? I can't take it with me," Edith replied, relishing Gail's annoyance.

As the car came to a full stop in her driveway, Edith opened her door and started walking toward her house. Gail caught up at the front porch. "Thank you for a most informative afternoon." She was about to close the door, but caught the determined expression on Gail's face. Like it or not, Gail wasn't going to let this go. "Join me for tea, won't you, dear? We need to talk."

In the familiar sanctuary of her kitchen, Edith brewed a pot of tea with herbs gathered from her garden while Gail set cups, sugar, and a tin of cookies on the breakfast room table. Sipping the fragrant beverage, Edith picked up the picture of her sons.

Frankie, her first-born, had been such a cute little boy. How had the ditzy flower child he married all those years ago become Gail, the controlling gorgon? Retired, Frankie now devoted his time to shaving strokes off of his golf score and researching a book about an obscure Civil War battle. The scar on his left cheek, still visible a lifetime later, summoned memories better forgotten.

"I don't believe we've ever spoken about Frankie and his brother's father," Edith said stroking the picture frame.

"Frank told me he died at Pearl Harbor. He didn't know much else." Gail sipped her tea. "This is very good."

Edith nodded. "My wedding to handsome young naval officer Jake Whitcomb was the talk of Norfolk society in June of 1940. 'Edith Tate, with her copper hair and violet eyes, was a stunning bride in white silk and antique lace,' the society editor said." She paused, nibbled on a cookie, and then squared her shoulders as if reaching a decision.

"I'm sure you were a lovely bride," Gail said.

"The trip to Jake's duty station in Hawaii doubled as our honeymoon. We took a train to California, followed by a cruise to the islands. If a photograph had been snapped of me boarding the ship in California, it would have captured a beautiful, carefree young woman smiling at the camera. Thankfully, there was no picture of the hollow-eyed girl who hobbled down the gangway in Hawaii, robbed of all innocence after Jake exercised his marital rights with a brutality unimaginable to an innocent young girl."

Gail's eyes widened as she grasped the meaning of her mother-in-law's words. "I am sorry."

"Lessons learned in finishing school taught me how to avoid the wrath of the more ambitious wives grappling to help advance their husbands' careers in a peacetime navy. And it was mostly a pleasant life in a tropical paradise." Edith settled back in her chair relieved to be telling her tale.

Gail sipped her tea, paying close attention.

"To my delight, Jake was at sea for weeks at a time. The life he planted in me on the ocean voyage—Frank—was a comforting companion. We hired a local girl as a maid who not only brought me herbs to ease the morning sickness, but others to enhance the flavor of our food. She taught me how to use just the right amount for maximum effect. The tropical flowers that surrounded me ignited my lifelong passion for plants."

"Really?" Gail said. "I didn't know that."

"Frank was born in March while Jake was at sea. A baby nurse, the maid's cousin, helped me recover from the birth. Talk of war was in the air, but I paid little heed. President Roosevelt would keep America out of any fighting. I was so naive." Edith lifted a spoon and stirred some sugar into her tea. "Jake returned from a long cruise in late May. He barely glanced at his firstborn before forcing himself on me. When he was spent, I poured whiskey until he passed out, and then tended to the baby and my bruises. Jake was absent most of that summer, home just enough to 'lay the keel,' as he put it, on his second son, Tom."

"I never knew," Gail said.

Edith continued. "Anxiety about war waxed as the year waned. One afternoon in September, Jake lined up old bottles behind the house and taught me how to shoot. At first the pistol felt awkward and hard to control, but I soon got the hang of it. I liked the sense of power it gave me."

"You shot a gun?" Gail blurted out, frowning with disapproval.

"Oh yes. Jake was pleased at my skill. 'You're a natural,' he told me. 'You must be able to protect yourself.' There was a lot talk about Japanese sleeper agents hiding within the local population, planning to defile white women. He meant that I should shoot myself rather than be ravaged by the enemy."

"Wow," Gail whispered.

"I was skeptical. My baby nurse and maid were third-generation Japanese who loved baseball and, as I learned on the Fourth of July, knew all of the words to all of the verses of the Star Spangled Banner. Jake returned at the end of November, after nearly two months at sea, craving sex and liquor. He drained the bottle of bourbon, but stayed conscious long enough to painfully claim his rights. Afterwards, I threatened to tell my doctor and Jake's superior—that cooled his ardor for a while."

"How awful," Gail stammered.

"Jake was charm personified at the officer's club that Saturday evening. He drank so much that he could barely walk. I drove home and left him in the car to sleep it off. Frankie's cries woke me early the next morning. I nursed the baby and watched the sun rise. The zoom of airplane engines shattered the peaceful dawn. Aerial maneuvers were common, but not on Sunday mornings. And then came the explosions, followed by plumes of smoke and flames in the distance. I knew it was no drill." Edith gazed over Gail's shoulder as though looking at something long ago and far away. "I wrapped the baby in a blanket, grabbed the gun out of a drawer, and ran to the car where Jake was still unconscious. He pushed me away when I tried to wake him, so I put Frankie in the back seat and slid behind the wheel. We were halfway to the base by the time he woke up. The roar of plane engines overhead was deafening, but Jake did not seem to realize what was happening.

"'Where are we going? You're driving too fast,' he yelled as I floored the accelerator. When I slowed for a curve, he slammed his foot on the brake, stalling the car.

"I shouted over the din, 'What are you doing? You need to get back to your ship!'

"'You need to give me a proper send-off!' He pulled my face toward his lap.

"'Are you insane? There's no time for that,' I shouted.

"'You're my wife and you will do what I say.'

"As he gripped the back of my neck, Little Frankie started wailing in the back seat. Jake released me long enough to backhand the baby, his academy ring slicing through his tender cheek, giving him that scar. Trying to right myself, I felt the familiar shape of the pistol under the seat."

Edith paused to sip her tea. "Two days later they notified me that Jake's body had been found at the back gate of the base near the body of a Marine sentry, both riddled with enemy bullets."

"How awful."

Edith took off her glasses and wiped the lenses with her napkin. Her eyes were dry.

"Tom's birth was so difficult, it prevented me from returning to the mainland with the other dependents. The boys and I didn't come back to Virginia until early 1945."

"You must have been relieved to be back home."

"My mother wasted no time finding me a new husband. Arthur, seventeen years my senior, was an executive in a local bank whose bad eyesight and flat feet had kept him out of the military. He was polite, shy, affluent, and mesmerized by what he called my 'russet tresses.'" Edith made air quotes.

Gail shifted in her seat.

"Our brief New York honeymoon was long on sightseeing and short on connubial activities—Arthur spent most of his time brushing my hair and muttering about its cinnamon color. The boys and I settled into the old, dreary house Arthur inherited from his parents. He was pleased when I was invited to join a garden club; he thought I would make social connections befitting the wife of a bank executive. I just wanted to hone my knowledge of herbs and plants. Arthur's feeble efforts at fatherhood evaporated when Frankie and Tommy showed no interest in his stamp collection."

Edith refilled Gail's cup and fiddled with the sugar bowl. Gail eyed her mother-in-law over the rim of her cup until she resumed her narrative.

"We'd just marked our first anniversary when Jake's mother died and left money to Frank and Tom. Without telling Arthur, I opened accounts for each of the boys in a savings bank that offered higher interest rates than Arthur's bank. When he found out, he was furious that I'd 'acted behind his back,' then shouted that I was too stupid to make financial decisions. Arthur succumbed to a fatal heart attack on the sixth tee at the country club that very spring. My fox gloves were spectacular that year." Edith smiled at the memory.

Edith paused staring into her teacup. "Arthur was leveraged to the hilt, even mortgaging the house to cover his bad investments, so I was left with nothing but a thin gold wedding band. We moved back with my parents, and I took a job in a local college library."

Edith rose from her chair, left the room, and returned carrying a large framed photograph of a pleasant looking young man with curly hair and wire-rimmed glasses. She placed in on the table, gently stroked the face, and smiled.

Gail recognized the picture. "Your husband, Henry, as a young man."

Edith smiled and nodded. "One snowy morning, a man in his thirties with a hitch in his gait, requested an obscure engineering reference book. It took a while to find because it had been misfiled on a dusty shelf in the basement. He thanked me and spent hours poring over the book and making copious notes. Two days later, he came back, asking for another technical book, which I found easily. When he came back a third day, I asked what he was up to. He told me that his name was Henry Beadle and that he had earned an engineering degree from the college in the late thirties. Like most men in his generation, he'd gone to war soon after, leaving part of his foot on a hillside in Italy. He worked at the shipyard and had an idea for a new kind of switch. He hoped to patent his invention and wanted to make sure it worked before he hired an attorney."

Edith rested her chin on a hand, lost in happy recollection.

"One day, while searching for something else, I found a book that I thought might apply to Henry's switch theory, and set it aside for his next visit. 'This is just what I was looking for, but didn't know it,' he said when I showed him the book. He took it to a table and spent the rest of the day taking notes. I stood behind his chair just before the closing chime so he could work until the last minute. When the end of day sounded I tapped him on the shoulder. Flustered, Henry thanked me, gathered his papers and left. He was back when the doors opened the next morning, and I had the book waiting for him on the counter. He apologized for treating me brusquely and keeping me from getting home to my husband."

Edith caressed the thick gold band on her left hand.

"I wore Arthur's ring to discourage suitors and remind myself that I was done with men, but I explained to Henry that I was widowed and my sons had been at a Scout meeting.

"Two days later, he asked if the boys and I would like to go to the circus with him. 'It's the least I can do to thank you for your help,' he said. Henry and the boys took to each other right away. I hadn't realized how much they needed a man in their lives and began to wonder if I did, too. That trip to the circus led to Saturday movie matinees, outings to museums, and, as the weather warmed, baseball games and the ocean. Henry became a regular at Mother's Sunday dinner table. I enjoyed being with Henry and liked how he slipped his arm around my shoulders sometimes," Edith said, touching her shoulder as if searching for Henry's familiar hand.

"Tom settled things one summer evening when a trip to the beach was cut short so Henry could get home to prepare for work the next day. 'Momma, why don't you just marry Henry so he can live with us?'

"I blushed with embarrassment. Henry said 'Why not indeed. Momma? Will you marry me?' and slipped to one knee. I could only nod. He finally kissed me—it was well worth waiting for."

Gail sighed. "How romantic."

Edith beamed at the recollection. "We were blissfully happy. Henry patented his switch and several other arcane but lucrative devices. Not for lack of trying, we never had a child together. As you know, Henry was a wonderful father to the boys. He felt fortunate to have survived the war and considered it an honor to raise Jake's sons in his place. I never told anyone else the truth about my first husband."

"Why are you telling me all this now?" Gail asked.

"It's time someone knew the whole story. As you recall when he turned fifty, Henry declared that he'd made enough money for one lifetime and retired. We traveled a lot and visited many parts of the world, but never Hawaii. Then, after nearly forty years of wedded bliss, cancer darkened our door."

"That was a hard time for all of us," Gail wiped away a tear. "I'll be right back, my heart pills make me need to pee all the time." She headed for the powder room.

Edith realized that it was a day very like today when she gathered ingredients for a special tea for Henry. He had been too weak to hold the cup but smiled as she held it to his lips. When he'd finished, she crawled into bed and held him in her arms until he fell into his final slumber.

Edith emptied the teapot into her cup, rose, turned up the kettle, and rummaged in the back of the cupboard for a different container of herbs. She measured those into the pot and filled it with hot water.

"You've done a good job keeping the house updated. It will show well. You could be out by summer," Gail said as she sat down. "Mother, don't make this difficult for everyone. We don't want to go to court to invoke your power of attorney, but it is time for you to move to a place where you'll be well cared for. It's not safe for you to live alone anymore."

Edith ignored the comments and refilled Gail's cup.

"There is so much of Henry here that I never feel truly alone. The night before his memorial service, I worked the contents of his urn into the soil around my prize camellia. Maybe that's why it weathered several hurricanes and recent bitter Virginia winters. Bone meal was interred in the columbarium the next day. This is my home, Gail. I will die here and join Henry under the camellia." Edith did not add that she believed she would join Henry in the not too distant future.

"But you can't do that," Gail sputtered.

"I can and I shall. I named Phoebe as my executor. She will inherit the house and carry out my wishes. Drink up, dear."

At a loss for words, Gail drained her cup then gasped. She clutched her chest as her eyes rolled back in her head.

Edith pulled her phone from a pocket, tapped 9-1-1 into the keypad, but did not hit send.

Her eyes drifted to the picture of her young sons as the rest of the story of "the day that will live in infamy" rose from the depths of memory.

"Gail, there's more to Jake's story."

Gail pressed a hand to her damp forehead. "Really?"

"I drove to the gate guarded by a very nervous Marine. He was distracted by the bombers flying overhead, and it took him a minute to process scene before him. A convertible driven by a pregnant woman in a bathrobe, a little boy bleeding from a deep cut on his cheek in the back seat, and a man—an officer by his uniform— slumped against the passenger door with half of his head missing."

"What the—?" Gail said.

"I begged the guard to do something!" Edith said. "But when he opened the door, Jake's body fell to the ground. I could tell by his expression that he knew that head wound had not been caused by a bullet from the sky."

"You shot him." Gail's words slurred.

Edith smiled. "I told him to never marry a redhead as I sped off. In the rearview mirror, I saw the enemy plane bear down on him."

Gail slumped forward, her breathing ragged.

"You know stress didn't cause my second husband's heart attack." Edith waited several more minutes and then tapped the send button on her phone. "Please send an ambulance. I think my daughter-in-law is having a heart attack."

After reciting her address, Edith finished her tea and went to the door to wait for the first responders.

ART ATTACK

HEATHER WEIDNER

"Move the amethyst goblet more to the left," gallery owner and curator, Harvey Owens, demanded, pointing to the right.

Jillian Holmes, Harvey's personal assistant, was balanced on a ladder in front of the glass cabinet. "Better?" She slid the goblet about four inches to the right and farther away from three green urns.

"I liked it better where she had it before," said Ilsa Prescott, owner of the featured glass and stoneware collection. As she stepped nearer to the display and shook her head, her silver bob shimmered under the gallery lights.

"Here, let me do it." Harvey hardly waited for Jillian to step down from the ladder before he moved the goblet back to where it was originally. "Hand me the green urns," he said, snapping his fingers. "

"Be careful with those, Harvey!" Ilsa shouted. "Those pieces are the cream of my collection. My late husband and I bought them on our travels and I expect them back in one piece after the exhibit ends."

"Thank you for reminding us again that you loaned them," Harvey said peevishly.

"They are the perfect addition to your gallery opening on Friday," Ilsa added.

"Right along with Da'rel's collection of acrylics and Marilyn Culpepper's watercolors," he countered.

"Your entire collection is lovely," Jillian added. "But that goblet is especially stunning—the way it fades from purple to violet to white. And that metal filigree design of wolves and the moon—gorgeous!"

"That's the blood goblet," Ilsa said. "My husband and I acquired it from a dealer in Romania. The dealer said whoever drinks from it and has an impure heart will be cursed. Those who drink and have reckless courage will be gifted with abundant success and great wealth."

Harvey rolled his eyes.

Ilsa winked at him. "It worked for me. It's my good luck charm. And my favorite piece."

Unconvinced Harvey turned to Jillian. "Hand me those ruby-colored flutes. I want them under the blood goblet."

"They look so gothic and magical." The comment came from behind them. Angie Webb, the receptionist, hung over her circular desk for a better view of the display. "I can't keep my eyes off all the pieces. The lighting is perfect over there."

"I'm hoping your guests will enjoy them as much as I do. I'll see you all on opening night." Ilsa slung her Gucci purse over her shoulder and tossed a wave at Harvey and his staff.

Just as the older woman stepped toward the gallery door, Marilyn Culpepper, the featured artist barreled in, pushing the door with enough force for it to hit the jamb. The rotund woman waved several sheets of paper at Harvey and said, "I need to see you about this. Now!"

"I'm working here, Marilyn," Harvey said. "Can't whatever it is wait?"

Jillian shelved a set of Ilsa's delicate perfume bottles and crystal decanters.

"No, it most certainly cannot," Marilyn sputtered. "These figures you sent me for last month's sales and consignments are off. You sold four of my large paintings, and your report shows only three."

"I'm sure it can be explained. Step into my office, and we'll look at it."

"Harvey, I'm getting tired of this," Marilyn said. Her voice got louder as she shook the papers again at the portly gallery owner.

He grabbed them, licked his fingers, and paged through them. "Come with me."

"This is the second time that the numbers and your checks have been off. I seriously doubt you want me to spread the word that you cheat artists. Richmond is a close-knit art community. We all talk to each other."

Ilsa Prescott frowned and slipped out the front door. Harvey followed Marilyn to his office and shut the door.

Jillian closed the ladder and stuck it in the corner. While she was putting the finishing touches on Ilsa's stoneware display of fiery orange and red sunset-patterned plates, Harvey's door burst open. Marilyn stormed out through the gallery and slammed the front door. Angie Webb raised her eyebrows and returned to the papers on her desk.

Harvey strode out of his office and stopped in front of the glass cases on the long wall of the main gallery in the refurbished antebellum warehouse. He looked transfixed by the glassware exhibit.

"Everything okay with Marilyn?" Jillian asked.

"That old bat has a greater sense of her talent than actually exists. It was just an accounting error. I don't know if we'll show any more of her stuff here." He started rearranging the plates and cups on the first shelf. Then he snapped his fingers. "Ladder."

Jillian dragged the stepladder back in place. He climbed up and rearranged the goblets. Green, red, and royal blue gemstone-colored glasses surrounded the blood goblet. He picked up the amethyst one again and admired it under the spotlight. He turned it around and tilted it to catch the light. Harvey looked mesmerized by the Romanian glass.

"Harvey. Harvey!" Angie called out from the reception area. "Kathy from the catering company is on line one. She wants the final count on the attendees for the opening. And she needs a check to cover the balance."

He put the glass back and climbed down the ladder. "I'll take it in my office."

* * * *

The next morning, Jillian found Angie standing on the sidewalk in front of the gallery smoking. "Morning. How are you?"

"Dreading the exhibit tonight. There is still so much to do and it looks like the rat bastard isn't even here."

"Does that surprise you?" Jillian asked.

"We don't need him anyway. You're the one who holds everything together around here. Ol' Harvey would be in a world of hurt if you ever left." She dropped her cigarette on the sidewalk and crushed it with her pointy-toed shoe.

"Thanks. I want to learn everything I can while I'm here. I want to be a curator someday." Jillian unlocked the door.

"It looks like Harvey ran off and left the lights on again," Angie said as she dumped her purse and coffee mug on the counter. "This place is a wreck. People—even the rich ones—are slobs."

"Harvey. Hey, Harvey!" Jillian yelled. She walked through the gallery and pushed open the partially shut door to his office. A foul stench smacked her in the face.

Stepping inside, she covered her nose with her hand. She jumped when she spotted two thick legs on the floor jutting out from behind Harvey's desk. Her stomach did a flipflop. "Angie, call 9-1-1!"

"What's going on?" Angie stuck her head in the office and immediately raised her fingers to her nose. "What died in here? Oh, crap. Is he okay?"

"I don't think so," Jillian said.

Jillian stepped closer to the body and the smell, a mixture of bodily fluids and stale alcohol, caused her stomach to roil. A puddle of congealing dark vomit surrounded the body, and a coffee mug and its contents lay beside him. Harvey's bloated face and hands made it look like he'd been in a fight, but the red and purple splotches on his cheeks hinted that it was something else. His swollen tongue lolled out of the side of his mouth like that of an elderly dog.

Harvey, what happened to you last night?

The question barely formed in her head when Angie snapped a picture.

Jillian glared at her. "What are you doing?"

"I watch *CSI*," Angie said. "I want to show the police how we found him. He's on his side like he fell out of his chair—covered in a mess of yuck." She punched numbers in her phone.

Jillian's heart pounded, and her knees felt weak as she stepped out and took a couple of deep breaths in the gallery. She dialed 9-1-1, reported their find to the police.

Angie followed. "Who else do you think we should call?"

"Ilsa Prescott is Harvey's landlord and silent partner," Jillian said.

"Wonder if we'll still have jobs?" Angie asked.

They stood in the doorway for several minutes until they heard sirens blare louder and louder. Two police cars and an ambulance parked in front of the gallery.

The first EMT jumped out of the ambulance with his bag. "Where is the patient?"

"In the office. Behind the desk." Jillian pointed toward the back of the gallery.

The EMTs scrambled inside, and the two police officers followed closely behind.

A few minutes later, both officers returned to the main gallery. One spoke into his shoulder mic. The other said, "I'm Sergeant J.T. Mason. Officer Ridgely and I will take your statements."

Officer Ridgely stepped toward Angie and the oval receptionist's desk while Sgt. Mason and Jillian stood near the front door.

"Your name and relationship to the gentleman in there," Sgt. Mason said as he nodded his head toward the office.

"I'm Jillian Holmes, Harvey Owens' personal assistant. Harvey's the curator of this gallery."

"When was the last time you saw him?"

"Last night. We are getting ready for a big art opening. We left about eleven thirty or eleven forty-five last night. Harvey stayed behind, but he wanted Angie and me to come in early to finalize details."

"Was he with anyone?" The officer jotted notes in a small black notebook.

"I don't think so," Jillian said.

"I'm going to need a list of everyone that was here yesterday and last night."

"We had a lot of people coming and going yesterday."

"Any security cameras?"

"The unit is in Harvey's office. He has a couple of cameras in here and one outside over the back door."

"Do you have contacts for his next of kin?" the sergeant asked.

Jillian nodded and said, "And his partner, Isa Prescott."

"Is there anyone who would like to see him hurt?"

Jillian hesitated. "He wasn't always the most popular person. He was pretty well known on the Richmond art scene, but there were people he had conflicts with. Let's just say he was abrasive. He had a loud discussion yesterday with an artist about money."

The sergeant frowned. "With whom?"

"Marilyn Culpepper," Jillian said.

"Are you two the only employees?" Sgt. Mason asked.

Jillian nodded as the EMTs navigated a gurney through the gallery to the office.

"Did he act concerned, angry, or depressed lately?"

"Not really. He was short-tempered most of the time and had dust ups with some of the artists or vendors. I don't think any of the arguments were ever serious."

"Can you get me those names and a list of your regular artists?"

Jillian nodded and stepped behind Angie's desk for pen and paper. She reached for the laptop to get the contacts.

Sgt. Mason held up his hand. "Wait. Leave that there until forensics has a chance to look at it."

"Okay."

Angie said, "Anyone want coffee? I can make some."

"No," said Officer Ridgely. "We want to look over the entire property, so I need you two to stay here until everything's cleared. Please don't touch anything."

A forensic team entered through the front. The first one went through the door, nodded at Sgt. Mason and headed toward Harvey's office.

"Stay here," Sgt. Mason said and followed the forensic team to the next room.

An hour later, the three EMTs wheeled the gurney out with Harvey's swollen body under a white sheet.

"Did you see that?" Angie whispered. "Harvey's really dead. Do you think they suspect us?"

"What? No."

"I guess I shouldn't mention to the police that I wished him dead a thousand times. And now that it's happened, I'm kind of in shock," Angie said.

Jillian glared at her.

"The cops asked me if Harvey had any enemies or people he had altercations with," Angie said. "He wants me to make a list of people who didn't like him. Who has time to put that kind of list together? It would be book size."

"I guess we hang out here until they're done," Jillian said. "I'm going to put a closed sign on the door."

The morning crept into early afternoon as the young women watched the forensic team meticulously move from Harvey's office to the kitchen area and the galleries. Jillian logged into the laptop for one of the technicians, and he downloaded files on a thumb drive.

Around three o'clock, the team packed their evidence gear and other equipment and left. Sgt. Mason strode to the reception area, and Angie put down her phone as he approached.

"The forensic team has finished its work here," Sgt. Mason said. "I'm turning the site over to you. Call whomever you need to and figure out your next steps. You will probably want to get a cleaner in here that specializes in disasters. Here's my card. Call me if you think of anything relating to Mr. Owens' death."

"Thank you," Jillian said. "What happened to him?"

"The autopsy will reveal the cause. There were no visible gunshots or stabbing wounds. I would call it suspicious for now."

After the two officers left, Jillian said, "I should call the Ilsa and find a cleaner. I need to stay busy."

"I probably should start polishing the ol' resume," Angie said. "I'm going to grab some food. Do you want me to bring you something back?"

Jillian's stomach growled. "Yep. A burger or a sandwich, please."

By the time Angie returned with Styrofoam containers from the deli down the block, Jillian had contacted Ilsa and found a cleaner. After they ate the late lunch, Jillian disposed of the empty cartons just as Ilsa appeared.

"Thank you coming over so quickly," Jillian said. "Right now, that room is kind of a biohazard but the cleaners will be here tomorrow. The police and the forensics team have searched every inch of this place."

"I'm still stunned at Harvey's death. I've been on the phone with the police for hours." Ilsa looked around the gallery. "Thank you both so much for taking charge and staying during all the chaos. I appreciate all that you do for the gallery. I know you two are the reason the gallery is a success. I'd like to talk to you all about running the gallery."

Jillian took a deep breath and nodded. "Thank you so much for the confidence you have shown in us. It would be my pleasure to run the gallery."

"And Angie, your job is also secured."

"Thank you." Angie sighed.

"What did the police say?" Jillian asked.

"The sergeant said that he is waiting on the autopsy results before he can determine if someone did harm to Harvey or whether he did it to himself. They guessed that it was some sort of poison," Ilsa said as she shifted from one foot to another. "Until we know exactly what it was, I would recommend cleaning out the kitchen and not using anything that's been opened."

"Are you serious?" Angie blurted out. "Someone could have tried to poison all of us?"

"Doubtful, but we don't know yet," Ilsa said. "The police have released the site, but I wouldn't take any chances."

"I'll clean out the kitchen tomorrow," Jillian said.

"Good," she said. "Let me know if you need anything. Let's say we all meet here on Tuesday at ten. We'll go over the books and the event schedule for the next quarter."

"Sounds like a plan," Jillian said. "I'm looking forward to it."

"Before I leave, Jillian, I want to tell you that I think you did a wonderful job with this display. It highlights my collection superbly, especially the blood goblet. You've got an eye for art," she said as she pointed to the glassware and the stoneware below it.

Jillian looked up at the blood goblet seeing it for the first time today. There was moisture on the glass and around the stem. It looked like it had been washed and put away damp. "That's odd. That's not how we left it last night," she mused.

"I love that goblet," Ilsa said. "It's irresistible to a specific type of man—the greedy and dishonest sort who see its legend as a challenge. It has been useful to me through the years. My husband, Ira, was drawn to it. He couldn't resist seeing if the legend were true. It was true—but not for him."

Jillian stared at her new boss. What was she suggesting?

"And now, it's worked its magic again, this time for both of us," Ilsa continued, smiling. "But you might want to wipe up that goblet and shelf yourself, and burn the rag. Harvey left a mess everywhere last night."

ABOUT THE AUTHORS

Frances Aylor, CFA, combines her investing experience and love of travel in her financial thrillers. *Money Grab* is the first in the series. www.francesaylor.com

Mollie Cox Bryan is the author of cookbooks, articles, essays, poetry and fiction. An Agatha Award nominee, she lives in Central Virginia. www.molliecoxbryan.com

Lynn Cahoon is the *NYT* and *USA Today* author of the best-selling Tourist Trap, Cat Latimer, and Farm-to-Fork mystery series. www.lynncahoon.com

J.A. Chalkley is a native Virginian. She is a writer, retired public safety communications officer, and a member of Sisters in Crime.

Stacie Giles lived many places before settling in Virginia where she is returning to ancestral Southern roots, including a grandfather who was a Memphis policeman.

Barb Goffman has won the Agatha, Macavity, and Silver Falchion awards for her short stories, and is a 23-time finalist for U.S. crime-writing awards. www.Barbgoffman.com

Libby Hall is a communication analyst with a consulting firm in Richmond, Virginia. She is also a blogger, freelance writer, wife, and mother of two.

Bradley Harper is a retired Army pathologist. *Library Journal* named his debut novel, *A Knife in the Fog*, Debut of the Month for October 2018. www.bharperauthor.com

Sherry Harris is the Agatha Award-nominated author of the Sarah Winston Garage Sale mystery series and is the President of Sisters in Crime. www.sherryharrisauthor.com

Maggie King penned the Hazel Rose Book Group mysteries. Her short stories appear in the *Virginia is for Mysteries* and *50 Shades of Cabernet* anthologies. www.maggieking.com

Kristin Kisska is a member of International Thriller Writers and Sisters in Crime, and programs chair of the Sisters in Crime—Central Virginia chapter. www.kristinkisska.com

Samantha McGraw has a love of mysteries and afternoon tea. She lives in Richmond with her husband and blogs at Tea Cottage Mysteries. www.samanthamcgraw.com

K.L. Murphy is a freelance writer and the author of the Detective Cancini Mysteries. She lives in Richmond, Virginia, with her husband, four children, and two dogs. www.Kellielarsenmurphy.com

Genilee Swope Parente has written the romantic mystery The Fate Series with her mother F. Sharon Swope. The two also have several collections of short stories. www.swopeparente.com

Deb Rolfe primarily writes mystery novels. This is her first published short story. She and her husband enjoy life in the Shenandoah Valley of Virginia.

Ronald Sterling is the author of six books and draws upon his colorful and varied life experience as a U.S. Airman, saloonkeeper, private detective, realtor, and New Jersey mayor.

S.E. Warwick, in the last century, earned a bachelor's degree in American Studies. Ever since, she has been trying to decipher the American enigma.

Heather Weidner is the author of the Delanie Fitzgerald Mysteries. She has short stories in the Virginia is for Mysteries series, *50 Shades of Cabernet*, and *To Fetch a Thief*. She lives in Central Virginia with her husband and Jack Russell terriers. www.heatherweidner.com

ABOUT THE EDITORS

Mary Burton is a *New York Times*, *USA Today*, and Kindle best-selling author. She is currently working on her latest suspense. www.maryburton.com

Mary Miley is a historian and writer with 14 nonfiction books and 5 mystery novels to her credit. www.marymileytheobald.com

Made in the USA
Columbia, SC
20 May 2020